ℓ
~P8/02

"Do you anticipate actually announcing an engagement?"

"I don't think we need to go that far," Caleb replied.

"So we're supposed to be living together with no intention of making it legal," Sabrina mused. "It's going to be bad enough having everyone think I've lost my mind enough to live with you. Having to explain that I was such a fool, I believed a diamond ring on my finger would tie you down..." Sabrina shuddered delicately.

Caleb grinned. "You're a woman in a thousand, Sabrina."

"And you," she said under her breath, "are certainly the man who's got enough experience to know."

D0365850

Hiring Ms. Right

Three single women, one home-help agency—and three professional bachelors in search of...a wife?

*Are you a busy executive with a demanding career?

*Do you need help with those time-consuming everyday errands?

*Ever wished you could hire a house-sitter, caterer...or even a glamorous partner for that special social occasion?

Meet **Cassie, Sabrina** and **Paige**—three independent women who've formed a business taking care of those troublesome domestic crises.

And meet the three gorgeous bachelors who are simply looking for a little help...and instead discover they've hired Ms. Right!

Enjoy bestselling author **Leigh Michaels's** new trilogy:

HUSBAND ON DEMAND #3600—On sale April 2000
BRIDE ON LOAN #3604—On sale May 2000
WIFE ON APPROVAL #3608—On sale June 2000

BRIDE ON LOAN
Leigh Michaels

TORONTO • NEW YORK • LONDON
AMSTERDAM • PARIS • SYDNEY • HAMBURG
STOCKHOLM • ATHENS • TOKYO • MILAN • MADRID
PRAGUE • WARSAW • BUDAPEST • AUCKLAND

If you purchased this book without a cover you should be aware that this book is stolen property. It was reported as "unsold and destroyed" to the publisher, and neither the author nor the publisher has received any payment for this "stripped book."

ISBN 0-373-03604-3

BRIDE ON LOAN

First North American Publication 2000.

Copyright © 2000 by Leigh Michaels.

All rights reserved. Except for use in any review, the reproduction or utilization of this work in whole or in part in any form by any electronic, mechanical or other means, now known or hereafter invented, including xerography, photocopying and recording, or in any information storage or retrieval system, is forbidden without the written permission of the publisher, Harlequin Enterprises Limited, 225 Duncan Mill Road, Don Mills, Ontario, Canada M3B 3K9.

All characters in this book have no existence outside the imagination of the author and have no relation whatsoever to anyone bearing the same name or names. They are not even distantly inspired by any individual known or unknown to the author, and all incidents are pure invention.

This edition published by arrangement with Harlequin Books S.A.

® and TM are trademarks of the publisher. Trademarks indicated with ® are registered in the United States Patent and Trademark Office, the Canadian Trade Marks Office and in other countries.

Visit us at www.eHarlequin.com

Printed in U.S.A.

CHAPTER ONE

THE calendar said it was Halloween, but Sabrina Saunders thought it felt more like the middle of March. The gray sky, pale daylight, low roiling clouds and howling wind made her think of the Arctic Circle in winter, not Denver on an October afternoon.

As she started to get out of her car, a gust caught at the convertible's door and slammed it against her shin. Sabrina winced in pain and paused to examine the leg of her silk trousers. Seeing that the edge of the door had hit hard enough to leave a streak of street dirt on the emerald-green fabric, she decided she didn't want to look at the damage underneath. There wasn't much she could do about it just now anyway.

She knelt on the driver's seat, propping the door open with one foot, as she dragged a couple of long, lightweight garment bags from the tiny back seat. The breeze whipped the flimsy plastic, and she tugged it away from her face as she hurried up the ramp at the front of the little bungalow to ring the bell. "Come on, Paige," she muttered as she waited, wishing she hadn't left her scarf and gloves in the car.

The door swung open, and Sabrina looked down at a white-haired woman sitting in a wheelchair. "Hi, Eileen," she said. "I brought Paige her Halloween costume for the party tonight. Is she here?"

Eileen McDermott didn't answer, just backed her chair out of the way, looked over her shoulder and called her daughter's name. Then she fixed her chilly gaze on Sabrina and said, "I do hope you're planning to close that door. I've already got a sore throat."

Sabrina bit her tongue to keep from saying how much she was enjoying the frigid air and finished untangling the end of one of the garment bags from the latch so she could close the door. "I'm sorry to hear you're feeling ill again, Eileen."

"I suppose I'm as well as can be expected," Eileen said with a long-suffering air.

Paige McDermott came around the corner from the kitchen, checkbook and pen in hand. "You're running a bit late, aren't you, Sabrina?"

"Just a smidge. Nothing I can't make up. And it was worth it, Paige, because look what I found today." Sabrina pulled up one of the plastic bags to show off the garment that hung underneath.

Eileen sounded as if she'd swallowed a lemon. "You can't mean that you chose *that* for Paige to wear at a children's party!"

Sabrina raised her eyebrows and looked thoughtfully from Eileen to the skimpy bit of midnight blue satin and lace she was holding at arm's length. "As a matter of fact," she said, "I think with her coloring she'd look lovely in it. If we team it up with some mesh stockings and very high heels, and maybe add a little ribbon tied around the neck—"

"Don't forget a long flannel bathrobe to cover up the goose bumps," Paige added.

"Made of a Scottish plaid, no doubt." Sabrina sighed. "Paige, do you have no sense of adventure? No romance in your soul?"

"Not a speck," Paige said firmly.

Sabrina ignored the interruption. "You'd look grand in

a satin teddy, and if the right guy was around you wouldn't have to worry about goose bumps, either.''

Eileen snorted. ''That's the kind of remark I'd expect from Cassie, not you. Now that she's gone all starry-eyed about that...that—''

''I believe the word you're looking for may be *man*,'' Sabrina said innocently. ''As a matter of fact, this bit of finery isn't for Paige. I bought it for Cassie. Saturday's her bridal shower, and I thought she'd rather have something like this than another casserole dish or set of tea towels.''

''And since you just happened to see it on the clearance rack as you were walking through Milady Lingerie...'' Paige murmured.

''Well, not exactly. At least, it wasn't on sale. But wait till you see what I *did* find on the clearance—'' Sabrina stopped. ''Hey, if you're implying I was goofing off, Paige, I wasn't. But Milady's right across the mall from the costume place, and I had to wait while they adjusted the tail on my cat suit.''

Paige laughed. ''And given a choice between killing time looking at lingerie or trying on clown noses—''

''I'll take lace and satin any day,'' Sabrina agreed.

Paige gave a tug to the other garment bag and glanced without apparent interest at the contents. ''At least it isn't lace and satin,'' she said. ''But I still don't see why we have to dress up for this. It's not like we're part of the party, we're just running the thing.''

''Because we won't look so out of place if we're in costume. And it'll be more fun for the kids that way. They love it when adults make fools of themselves.''

''No doubt,'' Paige muttered darkly. ''Personally, I wouldn't mind dressing as the party organizer. Jeans, sweatshirt, running shoes and clipboard are my idea of a great costume.''

Sabrina grinned. "Hey, be grateful I didn't call you All Hallows' Eve and deck you out in fig leaves and apples."

"I'll remember that," Paige said. "Mother, are you absolutely certain you don't want to go to the party at the senior center tonight instead of staying here alone? I can drop you off, and they'll make sure you have transportation home even if I'm late. It would be much more fun—"

"If you're worried about my safety, Paige, I certainly have no intention of opening the door to the sort of little hoodlums who are likely to come trick-or-treating. I'll just sit here with the lamps turned off, with my book and a flashlight, and they'll never know I'm home at all."

Sabrina wanted to roll her eyes. Sitting alone in the dark seemed to her to be one of Eileen's favorite pastimes— especially if there was a chance of making Paige feel guilty about it.

"Now if you wouldn't mind finding my cough drops, Paige," Eileen said.

"Is your throat worse, Mother?"

"I don't think so." Eileen's tone, in contrast to her words, was full of doubt. "Though if you *could* see your way clear not to go out tonight... Cassie will be there to help with the party, won't she?"

Sabrina nodded. "But it'll take all three of us just to oversee the people I've hired."

"I thought this was going to be a small party," Eileen said. "Just a little entertainment for the staff's children, to keep them off the streets on Halloween night."

"That's what I thought, too," Sabrina agreed. "But then it grew into a celebration for everybody at Tanner Electronics."

"That's because Caleb Tanner's bimbo of the week got hold of the idea," Paige explained.

"At least she's not expecting us to arrange all the entertainment for the adults." Sabrina wrinkled her nose at the memory. "But since it looks as if her festivity's going to last all night, I decided it might be prudent to hire a couple of baby-sitters for each age group, to take the kids off and entertain them while their parents party."

"It breaks my heart, Paige," Eileen said mournfully, "the sort of people you're being exposed to."

She sounded, Sabrina thought, as if she believed her daughter was still an impressionable preteen. "And there's an amazing age range on these kids," she went on, "so the number of sitters required—"

"Besides, there's not only a range, there's a lot of kids," Paige said. "For what was represented to us as a bunch of nerds with nothing on their minds but work, the crew at Tanner Electronics have an awful lot of offspring."

"Which is why it'll take all hands to manage the party, Eileen. And right now," Sabrina added, "though she means well and she tries hard, the fact is that Cassie doesn't have eyes for anything but Jake, so she's going to be of minimal—"

"That'll wear off soon enough." Eileen's tone was chilly. "The tunnel vision, I mean. And obscene bits of underwear won't delay the process by much, either."

Obscene? The teddy was certainly suggestive, Sabrina thought. It was even a trifle naughty—that was the whole point of honeymoon lingerie, after all. But it was hardly obscene.

Sabrina couldn't stop herself. She draped the teddy across the arm of Eileen's wheelchair so the woman couldn't avoid an up-close view while she painstakingly retied a blue satin ribbon, located at the bikini line, which had come undone. "I don't suppose you'd like to tell us exactly how you know all that," she said innocently as she held up the teddy once more.

Paige intervened hastily. "If you're going to get everything done in time, Sabrina, hadn't you better be going? I'll be along just as soon as I can."

"Perhaps you'd better go right now, Paige," Eileen said. Her voice was grim. "There's no telling what Sabrina could accomplish if she's left to herself—she could bring down the whole business that you've worked so hard to build."

"It is true," Paige said judiciously, "now that Rent-A-Wife has landed a client like Caleb Tanner, we'd be wise to avoid offending him. But I'm sure Sabrina already—"

Sabrina gave her a sunny smile. "Oh, well, if not offending Caleb Tanner is the goal," she said gently, "then you really had better wear the teddy!"

The atrium lobby at Tanner Electronics was brightly lit and bustling; Sabrina noted that Cassie's crew of volunteers had been busy, for most of the decorations they'd selected were already in place. Fake spiderwebs, bats hung on threads and a scarecrow-like witch in the corner all looked a bit obvious at the moment, but when night settled in and the lights were turned down, the effect would be appropriately spooky.

Not as good as a true haunted house, of course, Sabrina thought regretfully. But in the year since she and Paige and Cassie had combined forces to start Rent-A-Wife, they'd learned to work within all kinds of restrictions. And since this was the first good-size job they'd done for Tanner Electronics, it was more important, Paige had said, to pull off a simple, nice event that stayed well within the budget than it was to blow Caleb Tanner's socks off with an expensive gala.

At the time, Sabrina had agreed, but after her first encounter with Caleb's bimbo of the week, she'd had a change of heart. It was more likely, it seemed to her, that anything Rent-A-Wife came up with would look anemic to a man who was used to the celebrations thrown by a woman who obviously had no hesitation about spending his bank balance.

But Paige was right; there was quite a difference between the two situations. And it was too late for modifications now. They'd just have to impress Caleb the old-fashioned way.

Though it was an hour till the start of the party, Sabrina changed into her sleek black cat costume in the ladies' lounge before she started to fill the dozens of black and orange helium balloons that would finish off the atrium's decor. She knew from experience how easily time slipped by when she was busy and how hard it was to break away from a half-finished task, with party pressure already under way, to change clothes. This way, if the kids started arriving before she was finished, they'd think that helping blow up balloons was simply part of the planned entertainment.

Pumping helium into what seemed to be a million individual balloons was not Sabrina's idea of high enjoyment. By the time the first hundred were filled, tied and bobbing from a hook on the side of the rocket-shaped helium tank, she was reminding herself that the occasional tedium of her job was more than offset by the daily advantages of flexibility, frequent change and lack of pressure.

By the time the second hundred were finished, she was regretting that she hadn't kept her coat handy; the delivery company had left the helium tank right inside the main door, and every time an employee or visitor came in or out, Sabrina got a blast of chilly air. But since the tank was almost as tall as she was, at least twice as heavy and awkward to boot, she didn't have the option of moving it.

"At this rate," she mused, "even Eileen will have to concede me the title of sore-throat queen."

She decided to take a break from filling and started to

untangle the blown-up balloons from the hook on the side of the tank; she'd tie them into clusters so as soon as Paige showed up she could start placing them strategically around the atrium to complete the decorations.

And just where was Paige, anyway, she wondered. Kids in costumes were going to start drifting in at any minute.

Sabrina counted out fifteen balloons and began tugging them free from the anchoring hook on the side of the tank, intending to haul them out of the draft from the doorway so she could work more easily.

Her attention was focused on untangling the balloon strings, and when one unexpectedly gave way Sabrina took an unplanned step backward, directly into the doorway. Directly into a brick pillar—or at least that's what it felt like to Sabrina. Only there weren't any brick pillars in the atrium—and even if there had been, brick pillars didn't swear.

The impact jolted her, and fifteen orange and black balloons soared free from her grip and bounded to the high ceiling. Short of driving a fire-department snorkel truck into the building, Sabrina bet they'd stay up there till they withered with age. "Now look what you've done," she said, and turned to face the object she'd collided with.

He was a big man, lean but broad-shouldered and a couple of inches over six feet. His size seemed to be magnified by his attire—a close-fitting black-and-silver motorcycle suit, complete with a dark-visored helmet, which completely hid his face.

"Nice costume," she said almost automatically. "But you're a bit early. The kids' party won't actually start for half an hour or so, and the adult version won't get rolling till—"

"I'm not here for the party." His voice wasn't much

more than a growl. Or was she hearing the effect of the helmet?

"You mean you always go around looking like a cross between Don Quixote and a Hell's Angel?"

"I mean I was merely walking in with an armload of mail when I got tackled by—of all things—an ill-mannered cat."

"You'd better be referring to my outfit," Sabrina said pleasantly. "Because if you're accusing me personally of being an ill-mannered cat—"

"I'm not the one who called you Don Quixote."

Interesting, Sabrina thought. It almost sounded like he'd taken the Hell's Angel part as a compliment.

"Just look at the mess you made." He waved a black-gloved hand at the floor.

Sabrina looked down. What would have been a respectable pile of envelopes, catalogs and folders, probably a hundred in all, had scattered like a shotgun blast across the granite floor, some skittering as much as ten feet across the slick stone. "I'll admit to being a bit clumsy," she said. "Look, I'm sorry I didn't see you, but you must have noticed me. And you could have walked around me, you know."

"How? You're right in the middle of the doorway, as much in the way as it's possible to be. Can't that project be done somewhere else?"

"It could," Sabrina said, "if the delivery company hadn't planted the tank right here."

"It's on wheels."

"Yes, but wheels or not it's too heavy for me to move. If you'd like to lend a hand—"

He moved quickly for a big man, Sabrina had to give him credit for that. So quickly, in fact, that before she'd even realized what he intended to do, he had seized the tank and tipped it back, nudging the wheels into motion with the toe of his boot.

The bunch of balloons she'd tied haphazardly to the hook on the side of the tank floated loose. Desperate not to see the rest of her work escape to the ceiling, Sabrina made a wild leap for the trailing strings.

Her foot hit one of the scattered envelopes, which slid like an ice skate across the smooth floor. She missed the balloons, and her shoulder hit the top of the tank and over-balanced it. All three of them—motorcyclist, tank and Sabrina—spun out of control and hit the polished granite.

The crash echoed around the atrium for what seemed hours.

Sabrina lay still for a long moment, trying to gather her wits and catch her breath, afraid to open her eyes. She'd hit the granite with only a glancing blow, she knew—prob-ably because the motorcyclist's body had broken her fall. But what about him? If, in addition to her, the tank had landed on him—

After the echo of the crash died, all she could hear at first was a faint hiss. Was that him, or had the valve on the helium tank ruptured at impact?

She rolled clear and sat up. The hissing stopped. Now he was groaning—but that was good, wasn't it? At least he was alive, though it was hard to tell through the darkened visor of his helmet whether he was conscious or not.

Mixed with the groans, she began to make out words. He *was* conscious, she concluded. And—judging by his choice of vocabulary—he was not very happy. Well, she couldn't exactly blame him for being upset.

His muttering was getting louder, she noted.

"Excuse me," Sabrina said. "But the kids are starting to come in for this party, so if you could modify the lan-guage—"

He stopped talking for a moment, and even through the darkened visor there was no mistaking the glare he sent her way. "A bit clumsy?" he quoted grimly. "That's what you call a bit clumsy?"

"Wait a minute. You're not going to blame this on me when the whole thing was your fault."

"Mine?" His voice was little short of a howl. "I didn't knock over the damned tank!"

"If you'd just told me what you were planning to do, I could have gotten the balloons out of the way—and if you'd picked up the mail, my foot wouldn't have slipped."

"You mean, the mail *you* knocked on the floor in the first place."

Sabrina bit her lip. She couldn't exactly argue with that, so she decided it was safer to change the subject. "Here, I'll help you up."

"No, thanks. I'll get myself off the—" He shifted position as if to sit up and let out a yell of pain, twisting his body so he could clap both hands to his right knee. "I *can't* get up."

Sabrina felt the blood drain out of her face. She looked wildly around for help.

Though it felt like forever, it could only have been moments since the accident, for just now were people starting to cluster around them. A man moved through the crowd, edging between onlookers until he reached the center of attention and knelt next to the motorcyclist, and Sabrina loosed a sigh of relief at the sight of Cassie's fiancé.

Jake Abbott shot a questioning look at Sabrina as he reached down to release the chin strap on the motorcyclist's helmet. "What happened this time, Sabrina?"

"What do you mean, this time?" the motorcyclist said as Jake pulled his helmet loose.

Sabrina got her first good look at his face, but it didn't

tell her much. He looked vaguely familiar, and she thought that under normal circumstances he'd probably be quite good-looking. A lock of dark brown hair tumbled engagingly over his forehead, and any woman who needed mascara would have killed for his eyelashes—long, thick, dark and curly.

Of course, at the moment it was hard to tell, because the man's face was twisted in pain and sweat had broken out in big drops on his forehead.

"Is she in the habit of assaulting perfectly innocent bystanders?" he demanded.

Sabrina ignored him. "Thank heaven you're here, Jake," she said. "He fell, and—"

The man on the floor spoke through clenched teeth. "I did not fall," he said grimly. "Cat Woman there knocked me down. She's a menace—I think she's broken my knee."

"Let's not leap to conclusions, Caleb," Jake said. He released the zipper at the motorcyclist's ankle and gently folded back the tight-fitting suit.

Caleb, Jake had said.

Sabrina's gaze flew to the motorcyclist's face. Now that she'd heard his name and knew what to look for, she could see him more clearly. Sure enough, under the pain-twisted expression lay the handsome features of Denver's most famous entrepreneur.

Of all the people in the world she could have collided with, Sabrina had flattened Caleb Tanner. Electronics wizard, playboy millionaire...brand-new client.

Stunned, Sabrina stared at his exposed knee. The flesh was already so puffy it was no wonder he couldn't bend it. And much as she tried to convince herself she was seeing a shadow, she couldn't honestly deny that the joint was already bruising, as well.

In fact, his knee was starting to resemble one of the

multitude of black helium balloons that were now cheerfully bouncing against the ceiling.

Her stomach felt queasy. What was it she'd been thinking just an hour ago, about impressing Caleb Tanner?

Well, Sabrina told herself gloomily, it looked as if she'd impressed him, all right. In all the wrong ways.

Sabrina was still sitting cross-legged, almost stunned, on the cold granite floor when the paramedics came. She watched as they worked over Caleb, and for a moment, she hardly noticed the petite redhead in a milkmaid's outfit who stooped over her, holding out a headband to which a set of cat ears had been attached. The ears looked as if they'd been stepped on.

With a sigh, Sabrina reached up to take the ears, raising her gaze to her partner. "Thanks, Cassie. I hadn't even realized they were gone. They must have gone flying when I hit the floor." She poked the headband approximately into place atop her head.

Cassie pulled it loose again and turned it so the ears faced properly forward. "Are you okay? The ambulance crew is about ready to transport Caleb, but maybe they should take a look at you before they leave. Did you hit your head?"

"No. At least I don't think so. Oh, Cassie—Paige is going to kill me for this."

"For what? Assaulting a brand-new client? She won't if I have anything to say about it."

"You're a love, Cassie."

"Because I'm going to get you first," Cassie said lightly. "After all I went through to land this account, you treat the boss like a punching bag...."

Sabrina felt tears sting her eyelids.

"Hey, I'm teasing," Cassie said hastily. "In the first place, you obviously didn't do it on purpose."

"He thinks I did."

"Sabrina, a man who's in pain always looks for someone to blame."

The paramedics elevated the gurney in preparation for rolling it out to the ambulance, and the crowd shifted and moved back to give them room.

Sabrina's conscience nagged till she caught Jake's eye and offered reluctantly, "Should I come along? Since I know exactly what happened—"

Caleb raised a hand in a commanding gesture. "Don't you dare let her, Jake. If that woman gets into the ambulance, I'll *walk* to the hospital."

Sabrina felt like sticking her tongue out at him, but there wasn't much point; he wasn't in a position to see because the gurney was already rolling toward the door.

A small boy who was standing nearby, wearing a superhero costume, said, "Where's the blood? Isn't there going to be blood?" Disappointment dripped from his voice.

The door opened, and a whoosh of cold air surrounded Sabrina. Wearily, she forced herself to stand. The chilly granite had left her feeling stiff and sore, and for a moment she wondered if she should have let the paramedics look her over.

From the doorway came a feminine shriek. Only half-curious, Sabrina turned to look.

A princess in long, flowing robes and a faux medieval headdress was blocking the door, hands pressed to her mouth, staring at Caleb in horror. "What *happened*, darling?"

His tone was dismissive. "Just an accident, Angelique. Nothing for you to have hysterics over."

"Figures," Sabrina muttered. "For her, he's brave and

manly. A couple of minutes ago you'd have thought he was barely hanging on to life."

"There's no need for you to miss your party, Angelique," Caleb said.

"The party? Darling, surely you don't think I could possibly stay here and have fun while you're in agony!"

Beside Sabrina, Cassie muttered, "She will if she knows what's good for her."

The princess seized Caleb's hand as if she was daring anyone to remove her from his side. The gurney started to roll again, and she walked alongside.

"I don't need to be fussed over," Caleb was saying as the door closed behind them.

"Whew," Cassie said. "My guess is that will be the final straw. Angelique's time as bimbo of the week has just expired. Of course, it may take her a while to realize it, but—"

Sabrina frowned. "How do you know that?"

"Didn't you see the way he looked at her when he said she didn't need to have hysterics?"

"Yeah, I saw. It looked pretty mild compared to the way he'd been looking at me. It's my opinion you're suffering from wishful thinking, Cassie. Just because you don't like Angelique..." Sabrina sighed. "And I thought the biggest problem I was going to face tonight was having to apologize to Paige for baiting Eileen about your bridal shower gift."

Cassie opened her mouth, then obviously thought better of the question. "Let's get the party started," she said instead. "What's first? Bobbing for apples?"

Sabrina looked at the house, then at the number scrawled on the square of paper clipped to the convertible's visor. The address agreed, there was no doubt of that. But had

she written it down wrong? The last place she'd have expected the playboy millionaire to live was in a neighbor-
hood that had long since passed its prime.

In the strong morning sunlight, the three-story colonial
revival house looked nothing short of dilapidated. Its white
paint was alligatored; one faded green shutter hung at a
tired angle and another was gone altogether. The railing on
the small balcony above the pillared front porch was missing half a dozen balusters, and one of the pair of chimneys
looked as if it could benefit from a serious tuck-pointing.

As she looked at the address again, however, a truck
pulled into the semicircular driveway and parked directly
before the front door. Two uniformed men climbed out, and
a moment later they began unloading what looked like a
hospital bed.

Yeah, Sabrina told herself. Unlikely as it seemed, she
had the right place after all.

She squared her shoulders and gathered up a small,
bright-colored shopping bag and a sheaf of fresh fall flowers wrapped in cellophane. Caleb Tanner would probably
throw the contents of the bag in her face and use the sharp
flower stems to defend himself, she thought gloomily. But
she had to make the effort. Whether he was likely to accept
her apology wasn't the point; she still had to offer it.

She followed the bed to the front door and up two steps
onto a crumbling concrete porch. The door stood wide
open; a small, fussy-looking elderly man was just inside,
giving directions to the delivery men.

The bed crossed the wide hallway and stopped while the
men debated how to make it fit through a too-narrow door.
They tipped it on one side and pushed; a rail scraped the
door molding, and the little man held his breath until the
delivery men set the bed down and stood back to scratch
their heads and consider.

From the doorway on the other side of the hall, opposite the room where the bed was noisily being set up, a familiar feminine voice cooed. "Darling, are you absolutely certain there isn't anything I can do to make you more comfortable?"

Angelique, Sabrina thought. Cassie had been wrong; the bimbo's time in the sun obviously hadn't expired just yet.

Sabrina edged closer and peeked around the corner of the doorway. Beyond it lay a large living room with a high-beamed ceiling, two sets of French doors and a fireplace where a blaze crackled cheerfully. Over the back of a black leather couch, which sat directly in front of the fire, she could see just the top of Caleb's head.

Next to him, perched on the edge of the couch cushions, was Angelique. "If you're certain," she said, and leaned against him for an obviously intimate embrace.

Sabrina drew back into the hallway and debated her next move. Fortunately, the little man was too absorbed in watching the delivery crew to ask what she wanted.

Before Sabrina had made up her mind what to do, Angelique appeared in the doorway. "What are you doing here?" she asked suspiciously, eying Sabrina. "Not that it matters. Mr. Tanner is resting, so you'll have to go away. Jennings, take the things this woman has brought and see her out. I have an errand to run, but I'll be back in an hour to see how our invalid is doing."

Without another word, she paused beside the front door and waited until the little man opened it for her. Head held high, she swept out.

The little man closed the door and turned to Sabrina.

Just as he opened his mouth, the delivery men gave the bed a superhuman push. It went through the doorway, but it left four deep, raw, precisely parallel scratches.

The little man squeaked, almost as if the scratches had

been made in his flesh rather than in unfeeling wood, and stormed across the room, chattering almost incoherently.

The instant his back was turned, Sabrina ducked into the living room.

The first impression she'd gotten from her initial glimpse of the room, of size and light and perfect proportions, was modified on closer examination. The room's pale yellow paint was faded with age, except for spots here and there where artwork had obviously blocked the sunlight for years, and the carpet was almost threadbare.

She walked around the end of the incongruously modern black leather couch. Caleb, wearing a worn navy-blue jogging suit, lay with his right leg propped on a couple of pillows and strapped into a canvas-covered immobilizer, which stretched from mid-thigh to his lower calf. Nearby a pair of aluminum crutches leaned against a small table.

Jake had told her last night when he'd finally returned to the party what to expect. Still, the sight stopped Sabrina in her tracks. Her throat tightened. Very deliberately she looked away from the injured leg and focused on Caleb's face.

His eyes were closed, and he was a little paler than she'd expected him to be. But of course she was basing her assessment on photographs she'd seen, and she was assuming, because many of those pictures had shown the playboy millionaire in outdoor activities, that he'd sport a perpetual tan. But that wasn't necessarily so, she told herself, and so his lack of high color didn't mean he was still in pain from his injury.

"I thought I made it clear—" he said, and opened his eyes.

Sabrina braced herself.

Caleb pulled himself up a little higher. "I suppose you've come to assess the damage you did."

She bit her lip. "I've come to tell you I'm sorry for my part in the accident."

"Your part?" His gaze roved over her. "Well, it's just as well you showed up—because otherwise I'd have had to come looking for you. Figuratively speaking, of course, since it's apparent I'm not going to be able to move much beyond this couch for a few days, at least."

He sounded perfectly matter-of-fact, not in the least vindictive or threatening. And yet there was something about the tone of his voice that sent a trickle of fear oozing through Sabrina's bones.

"Yes," he said. Somehow he made the word sound almost triumphant. "You're just the person I've been wanting to talk to."

CHAPTER TWO

THE pillows supporting Caleb's knee slid, and the shaft of pain that shot up his leg made him wince and look hopefully at the clock. But there was another hour to wait before he could have the next dose of pain medication, so he swore under his breath, lay back as best he could, took a couple of deep breaths and tried to distract himself by studying the woman who stood beside the sofa.

Under normal conditions, he decided, she could take a man's mind off almost anything. Of course, these weren't normal conditions. His knee was a constant reminder that she was not only pleasant to look at but damned dangerous to handle—and that was something he had no intention of forgetting.

He'd noticed her as soon as he'd walked through the front door at Tanner Electronics yesterday, just as he noticed any extraordinarily pretty woman who happened across his field of vision. His optic nerves were hard-wired for that sort of observation, so in the first split second he'd automatically assessed the basics—she was tall and slim, with hair as sleek as black satin and green eyes set at an exotic tilt in a porcelain-fine heart-shaped face.

Then she'd pasted him to the floor, and suddenly he hadn't been in the mood to study her any further. He already had enough of a mental picture to let him identify her in a police lineup or to avoid her on the street, so what else could he possibly need to know?

But that had been yesterday. Since then, he'd had an unpleasant evening in the emergency room, a long and almost-sleepless night and an almighty frustrating morning. Now here she was again—and it occurred to him that he might be able to put Cat Woman to good use.

Though…it was mighty convenient of her to show up just now. Suspicion flickered through him. Was it possible she had some sort of agenda of her own?

He surveyed her through narrowed eyes and decided that she looked far too ill at ease to be plotting anything. Relieved, he dismissed the idea and settled back, letting his gaze linger on her face.

His initial assessment might have been lightning-fast, but it had been absolutely on target, he concluded without surprise. Where pretty women were concerned, he never missed.

Today the satiny hair was pulled into a subdued knot at the nape of her neck, and instead of the slinky black cat costume she was wearing a soft tweed pantsuit in a color that made him think of the pine forests that lined the foothills of the Rocky Mountains. Neither change did anything to diminish her attractiveness. They simply added an air of efficiency and capability.

Which just went to show, Caleb thought, how very deceptive appearances could be.

"Sit down," he invited, and waved a hand at a nearby chair.

She set the small shopping bag she carried on the floor near the couch, laid the sheaf of flowers on the coffee table and sank onto the edge of the black leather seat. To watch her, Caleb told himself, one would think she was the most graceful creature on earth.

"I brought you a few magazines," she said. "I hope they'll help pass some time." She seemed to be having trouble making her voice work right. "I understand your knee's not broken, after all, just sprained."

"Technically, they called it a strain." He saw the tiny quiver of relief go through her and added maliciously, "Of course, the doctors tell me a bad strain's almost worse than a break. It'll certainly take longer to heal completely, and it's far more likely to be reinjured in the future if I'm not extremely cautious."

"Oh." Her voice was very small.

"Yes. I'm looking forward—if you want to put it that way—to as much as two weeks in this contraption." He gestured at the immobilizer. "And even after that, I'll still be on crutches for a while. It will likely be months before I'm back in top form."

She'd turned white, he noted. Encouraged, he pressed on. "That means I can't easily go up and down stairs. I can go to work, but only if I install a recliner or a hospital bed in my office to keep my leg elevated. And of course, that's assuming I can get there—I couldn't drive a car even if I had one, and I certainly can't ride my motorcycle."

"If you're trying to make me feel bad, Mr. Tanner—"

"Not at all," he said, not even trying to sound candid. "I'm only telling you the circumstances of my life. The very much changed circumstances."

"I've already said I'm sorry."

He pretended not to hear. "You know," he said sadly, "I was scheduled to go skydiving this weekend."

Her eyes, he noted with interest, looked like turbulent storm clouds when she was angry.

She said, through almost clenched teeth, "Would you knock off the pity party?"

He stared at her and did his best to look wounded. "If you think I don't have a right to feel sorry for myself, Ms.—"

"Oh, you've got a right. I just don't think that's what

you're doing at the moment. If you're hoping to scare me into offering you some sort of settlement—''

''Not a bad idea,'' he said thoughtfully.

''For the damage I've supposedly done to you—''

''What do you mean, supposedly? This immobilizer isn't exactly a figment of my imagination.''

''There's still the question of who's really at fault, you know.''

''But there's no doubt at all about who's been damaged.''

''Nobody made you grab hold of that tank.''

''What? You asked me to lend a hand!''

''I didn't suggest you pretend to be Hercules. At any rate, I should warn you that I don't have much in the way of financial resources. So if you *are* hoping to collect from me, I'm afraid that you're not going to have much luck.''

Caleb shrugged. ''Money I have plenty of. But there are other ways of settling scores, you know. The kind of damages I want to collect, you'll have no trouble paying.''

Her eyes turned to arctic ice. The effect was almost enough to make him shiver.

''I see,'' she said. ''Of course, it wouldn't be the first time a man has leaped to the conclusion that because I'm not exactly hard on the eyes, it would be worth his while to try to manipulate me into bed, but—''

He grinned. ''You think sex is what I have in mind? When the moon turns to liverwurst, maybe.''

She colored a little and said in a small, tight voice, ''I do apologize. How conceited of me to assume you might find me attractive in that way.''

So the lady had a vulnerable spot, he thought with delight. ''That wasn't what you assumed,'' he said easily. ''You jumped to the conclusion I'm the kind of guy who wouldn't hesitate to blackmail a woman for sex whether I found her attractive or not."

Her gaze dropped to her hands, folded in her lap.

"Not a very flattering picture," Caleb went on. "But you know, I didn't say that I don't find you appealing. It's just that, having already had a good demonstration of what you're capable of, I'd have to be a blooming idiot to ask for more. Frankly, my mind boggles at the thought of what you could accomplish if—"

"There's no need to go into detail, Mr. Tanner. Now, since we've established that we're not discussing going to bed, perhaps you'd like to make clear what you do have in mind?"

He took his time. Letting her stew in suspense might have interesting results. "As I've already pointed out, there are a number of things I'm not going to be able to do on my own for the next few weeks."

"So? I presume that's why you have what's his name out there. Jennings—is that it?"

"Jennings is a fine butler in what has up till now been a low-maintenance household."

He watched her gaze flick around the room. "Are you sure low-maintenance is the word you want?" She sounded honestly curious. "I'd call it neglected, myself."

"I'm not referring to the house, exactly, but to my needs. Jennings answers the door and the telephone, cooks a bit, supervises the cleaning team, that sort of thing. But I take care of myself."

"Fancy that."

He decided to ignore the interruption. "However, now I can't look after my own needs—and I can't expect Jennings to pick up the slack. He's too old to be on call around the clock, but someone will have to be."

"And you're expecting me to wait on you?"

"You've got it. I'm going to need someone to fetch and carry, hand me my crutches, sort out my pills, plump my pillows, bring fresh ice packs, read to me when I'm restless, go out for ice cream at three in the morning if I can't sleep...."

"I get the idea," she said dryly. "I just don't see why you want me doing all those things."

"I'd say you're a natural choice. Jake tells me this is the very sort of thing your business does all the time."

"Not precisely," she said coolly. "There's a reason we called it Rent-A-Wife, not Buy-A-Slave."

"Look at it this way, Ms..." He shifted, trying without success to get more comfortable. "What *is* your name?"

"Does it matter? I thought slaves had to answer to whatever their masters called them." After a moment, though, her gaze wavered and she said softly, "Sabrina Saunders."

"Sabrina," he said slowly, making the name almost a caress. "You caused this problem. You're going to fix it. At least as much as it can be fixed."

"Look, there are agencies that provide special-duty nurses, and I'm sure you can afford to—"

"I didn't ask you for nursing services. I do not have a death wish. In fact, there are limits to slavery, too—I don't expect you to deliver hot soup directly into my hands. Having you set it on a table nearby will be risky enough, in my opinion."

"You know," she said slowly, "that's what I don't understand. I should think all you'd have to do is raise your voice and there would be a hundred women swarming around you, thrilled to be of service."

"Exactly." His voice was crisp.

She frowned. "Then I really don't understand why you're putting pressure on me. Why would you want a reluctant helper—one you don't even trust not to scald you with the first cup of coffee—when you could have enthusiastic ones?''

"Because I don't even have to raise my voice to attract all those women, that's why. I don't know if you ran into Angelique when you arrived?''

She sounded wary. "We spoke, yes. Actually, she spoke to me, but I didn't exactly answer.''

"She's been here since the crack of dawn. She'd have spent the night except that all she had to wear was the princess costume.''

"And you didn't like the idea of having *her* plump your pillows? I don't get it.''

"Plumping pillows was not the sort of thing she had in mind.''

"Ah,'' she said on a long note of discovery. "I suppose last night you weren't feeling up to any—how can I put this delicately?—athletic activity. Well, I can see how having a woman like Angelique around in those circumstances might make a man like you very uncomfortable, but—''

"And she's far from the only one who's been hovering helpfully. Since the word started to spread last night that I was injured, there have been seventy-two phone calls and nineteen visits from women.''

Sabrina shrugged. "Sounds like masculine heaven to me.''

"Not when I'm flat on my back and unable to defend myself. Every one of those women has ideas of mothering me, nursing me or otherwise convincing me that I simply cannot live without her on a permanent basis. In other words, they're far more interested in their left ring fingers than in my knee.''

"And you really don't believe you can defend yourself against that?'' She shook her head. "I'm disappointed in you.''

"I don't choose to spend my energy on that kind of battle. I'd rather focus it on getting back on my feet as soon as possible."

She'd gone straight on. "And you call yourself a play-boy! Besides, you have Jennings out there. All you have to do is tell him to turn off the phone and not let anyone in, and—"

"Oh, really? *You* got past him without any trouble, didn't you?"

She sounded a little less certain of herself. "You said you wanted to see me."

"But you didn't know that till after you were sitting here. And he doesn't know it yet. No—Jennings is well-meaning, but he's not cut out to be a bodyguard."

He watched the play of expressions cross her face. Now, he thought, they were getting somewhere.

"Face it, Sabrina—since it's entirely your fault that I'm being subjected to this siege, it's entirely your responsibility to do something about it."

She slapped her hands against her thighs and stood up. "You know," she said, "I think you're right. Goodbye."

Caleb blinked in surprise and tried to struggle into a sitting position. "Where do you think you're going?"

She barely paused. "To the animal rescue league to see if they happen to have a Rottweiler with misogynistic tendencies. I'll sign the adoption papers, deliver him to Jennings, and your problem will be solved by noon."

"Sit down, Sabrina."

"But it's the perfect—"

His voice was silky. "Let's talk about this business of yours."

"Rent-A-Wife? What about it?" She sounded ever so slightly apprehensive.

"Do you and your partners want to continue to work

with Tanner Electronics employees?'' He saw the flicker of discomfort in her eyes and smoothly pressed his advantage. ''Or shall we just call it one of those trial runs that unfortunately didn't work out?''

She stopped in mid-step. Very slowly, as if she were walking to the guillotine, she returned to her chair and sat down. ''When do I start?''

Satisfaction sizzled through Caleb. He hadn't realized that being on the receiving end of total capitulation could be so enjoyable.

''Right now will be fine,'' he said. ''But I hope you don't mind if we don't shake on the deal, Sabrina. I'm going to need the use of both hands, and I really don't want to take the chance of you messing one up.''

Sabrina's fingers moved automatically, arranging the sheaf of flowers she'd brought in a tall glass vase, while she told herself that of course she'd done the only thing she could.

Faced with the threat of Rent-A-Wife losing its newest and single most substantive client, she hadn't been left with much choice.

In fact, she thought, instead of growling over the idea of spending the foreseeable future waiting on Caleb Tanner hand and foot, she should probably be thanking her lucky stars that a maidservant was all he wanted. How stupid it had been to feel that flash of resentment at the idea that he didn't find her physically attractive—for even though he'd sidestepped the question, there was no doubt in Sabrina's mind that if he'd really found her desirable, he wouldn't have hesitated to act on that feeling.

Her irritation had been almost an automatic reaction, of course—the kind of thing she would probably have felt for an instant no matter who had made the statement. Her momentary fury really had nothing to do with Caleb Tanner.

In fact, she decided, it had nothing to do with men at all; it was more likely a psychological warning buzzer. If she couldn't laugh off the notion that a man—any man—might not find her appealing, then perhaps her ego was getting out of line and needed a serious pruning.

In any case, she should be celebrating the fact that Caleb hadn't tried to force her into his bed. Because if he had...

She squashed a momentary vision of Caleb Tanner's face looming above her, his handsome features honed by desire.

Rent-A-Wife would just have had to cope with the fallout of losing an important client, she told herself.

The loss would have been monstrously unfair to Paige and Cassie, of course, but there was nothing Sabrina could have done about that. And they would have understood; there were prices that no one should be expected to pay, and sleeping with Caleb Tanner was one of them.

Obviously there was no shortage of women who didn't agree with that philosophy, Sabrina admitted. But she'd never made a habit of following the crowd, and she wasn't about to start now just because Caleb was involved. The fact that there were women standing in line hoping to be his bimbo of the week was no recommendation where Sabrina was concerned.

However, it looked as if Cassie had been right, after all, when she'd said Angelique's time in the spotlight had expired. Perhaps the rest of the feminine crowd had sensed that Caleb was getting restless and ready for a change; that would help explain why women had started to swarm around him as soon as they'd heard he was hurt.

That thought provided a little comfort to Sabrina. Not that she much cared what happened to Angelique, but it gave her a little more hope for her own situation.

It appeared, from everything she'd ever heard about him, that Caleb Tanner was constitutionally incapable of sticking

with any one woman for long. Implying that whichever
lady he was currently seeing would last no longer than a
week might be a trifle exaggerated, but the description
hadn't come out of nowhere.

Therefore, Sabrina thought, it wasn't unreasonable to
hope that he'd soon get tired of her, too—or at least grow
weary of the idea of exacting revenge for his injury by
keeping her dancing attendance on him. And, wildly im-
probable though it sounded, if she was actually successful
in keeping all of his women away...

Well, Sabrina thought, he could talk all he wanted to
about not wanting them around, but she'd bet her convertible that Caleb would soon be bored without his harem. In
fact, she calculated, she'd give him three days maximum.

Feeling considerably more cheerful, she stuck the last
flower into the vase and was starting to wipe up the water
drops that had splashed everywhere when Jennings came
into the kitchen carrying a cordless phone, which he held
out to her without saying a word.

Sabrina took it and tried to brace herself. "Jennings, did
Mr. Tanner tell you to pass his calls on to me?"

"The lady asked for you, miss."

Relief whispered through her. "Oh, that must be my
partner. She wasn't answering her phone a few minutes ago
so I left a message on her voice mail." *And you're deliberately delaying,* she told herself, *because you aren't looking forward to reporting this morning's change of plans.*
"I'll be out of your way here in a minute, Jennings. Where
will I find the garbage can?"

He pointed at the far corner of the room. "I'll take care
of the debris, miss."

"Way over there? Why? It isn't even next to the back
door, much less convenient to anything else. I don't know
a lot about kitchens—"

Even though she hadn't yet put the phone to her ear, Sabrina could hear laughter from the other end of the line. She tucked the phone between shoulder and ear and said, with mock hauteur, "I don't recall asking for your opinion, Cassie."

"What you know about kitchens would fit on the head of a pin with room left over," said her unrepentant partner.

"That may be true. But I know an inefficient one when I see it."

"Whose kitchen are we talking about, anyway?"

"Well…this could require a bit of explanation." Sabrina took a deep breath. "It's Caleb Tanner's."

The long silence on the phone was the loudest Sabrina had ever heard. "No wonder the phone number looked vaguely familiar. Why aren't you using your cell phone, by the way?"

"It's not working. It seems to have been a casualty of the fall last night."

"That figures," Cassie said. "So about Caleb… Please tell me he invited you."

"No, Cassie, I crashed my way in." It was true, of course, but Cassie would never believe it—and what her partner didn't know, Sabrina told herself, wouldn't hurt her. "Actually, I came to apologize."

"So what's keeping you? Sabrina, do us all a favor and get out of there before something else happens."

"Now *you're* treating me like Typhoid Mary," Sabrina complained. "Honestly, Cassie, you make it sound as if I'm too clumsy to walk down the street and whistle at the same time!"

"You have to admit you're the only person in Denver who can fall over a ray of sunlight—I've seen you do it. Just don't take any chances, all right? Maybe you don't realize how important Tanner is to Rent-A-Wife right now, but I saw last month's profit-and-loss statement when Paige was working on it, and believe me, we can't afford to lose this client.''

"I know," Sabrina said quietly.

Cassie had gone straight on. "Plus, on a personal level, Sabrina, I'd kind of like to remain on speaking terms with my future husband's boss, so if you could avoid offending Caleb any further—''

Sabrina raised her voice. "He's asked me to help him out for a few days.''

"Help him.... You've got to be joking.''

"He can use a hand just now. Twenty-four hours a day, in fact.''

"Caleb Tanner wants you with him around the clock? What's the man taking for pain medication, and does his doctor know he's showing symptoms of psychosis?''

Sabrina went straight on. "So that means I can't handle my regular clients.''

"I suppose you want to pass them off to me? Sabrina, you know I'm only scheduled to work half days till my wedding—''

"What were you saying about the Tanner account being very important just now?''

Cassie swore under her breath. "All right, give me your list.''

Sabrina closed her eyes in relief. It was one small blessing—not so much for her sake but for Cassie's—not to have to give her partner every last detail. Why should both of them have the whole mess to worry about? "Thanks, Cassie. It's not that long a list, really. And I'll make it up to you, I swear.''

By the time she put the telephone down, Jennings was taking containers of food from the refrigerator, stacking them almost haphazardly on a tiny strip of countertop nearby. "Is there anything particular you'd like for lunch, miss?"

"Heavens, no. Don't go to any special trouble for me."

He caught a paper-wrapped bundle just as it slid off the pile. "I'd be happy to cook whatever you'd like. Of course, if you'd prefer to make yourself at home in the kitchen—"

Sabrina said hastily, "I'm not big on kitchens. Is this one really as inconvenient as it looks?"

"It's the worst arrangement I've ever seen, miss, but then there hasn't been time to do much about it. I expect when Mr. Caleb gets back on his feet, there'll be some changes."

"Then this house is a new purchase? That's a relief—I was thinking it might be the family homestead, handed down for generations."

Jennings almost cracked a smile. Sabrina felt rewarded.

"Oh, no, miss," he said. "Mr. Tanner's parents live in Boulder, and until last month he had an apartment in one of the new developments downtown."

"Really? But he moved here? Why?" Sabrina raised an eyebrow. "No, let me guess—I bet the landlord objected to the bimbos getting into a traffic jam in the lobby. Actually, it's too bad he didn't stay there, because the doorman could have doubled as a security guard." *And I'd have been saved a lot of trouble.*

An asthmatic-sounding chime wheezed from the front hall. *There's Angelique,* Sabrina thought. *She said she'd be back in an hour.*

It was apparent that Caleb had heard it, too. He called, "Sabrina! Come in here, will you? And bring Jennings with you."

She carried the vase into the living room, setting it with exaggerated caution in the precise center of the coffee table, just out of his reach. Then she picked up the motorcycle enthusiasts' magazine that had slid off his lap, gave it back and said, "What do you want me to tell Angelique?"

"Nothing. Just let her in, Jennings."

Silently, Jennings headed for the door.

"I thought you wanted me to defend you," Sabrina said.

"You're going to. Sit down. No, here on the floor right beside me, with your back to the couch."

She looked doubtfully at him, but there wasn't time to argue; she could hear the squeak of the front door opening. As Sabrina folded herself up on the carpet, she bumped the sore spot on her shin where the car door had caught her yesterday and grimaced.

"I see I'm not the only one who suffered damage in our collision," Caleb said. "You should have told me."

"Would it have made any difference in your demands?"

"Of course not. But we could have felt sorry for each other." He shifted onto his side and swore irritably. "Not being able to turn over without help is going to get mighty aggravating, you know." He draped one arm around her shoulders and slid the magazine onto her lap. They must look, Sabrina thought, as if he was leaning over her to point out something. It was a nice, friendly little pose....

"Darling," Angelique said, "I do hope you've gotten some rest, because—" She rounded the end of the couch and stopped dead in her tracks. "What in the—"

"Hello, Angelique," Caleb said calmly. "I'm glad you stopped in. Sabrina was just telling me a minute ago that she wished she could thank you properly for helping out this morning till she could get here. In fact, she said when this is all over, she'll throw a back-to-good-health party for me and invite you."

Angelique opened her mouth and shut it again.

Sabrina, half-stunned herself, had no trouble imagining what the woman was feeling.

"You can't mean this," Angelique said. "You can't toss me aside like this, Caleb. You need me, especially now...." Her voice trailed off.

His voice sounded oddly gentle. "I told you days ago that we were finished, Angelique. You wanted to follow through with the Halloween party since you'd gone to so much trouble over it, and I agreed. But the party's over, honey. And messing up my knee didn't change my mind."

Angelique's tone was suddenly venomous. "You didn't say anything about *her*."

"Surely you're not surprised. It would hardly have been respectful to drag Sabrina into it, because she didn't cause the breakup, you know. It was just time, Angelique."

"Of course she didn't cause it." Angelique's voice dripped sarcasm. "I'm sure she just happened to be innocently standing there when you started looking around." She glared at Sabrina. "Well, let me warn you, girl, you'll be just one more in a long line. Whatever he tells you, the truth is as soon as he's got what he wants, he'll start looking around again. So enjoy it while it lasts—because it won't last long." She tossed her long hair and stormed out of the room. The bang of the front door told Sabrina that this time Angelique hadn't waited to be respectfully bowed out.

Sabrina slammed the magazine down on the carpet with a satisfying bang. "That was the worst, most obnoxious, horribly callous piece of behavior I have ever seen."

Caleb leaned heavily on her shoulder in order to push himself into position on the couch. "Angelique isn't known for her tact, but I didn't expect she'd be quite so unrestrained. I'm sorry about that."

Sabrina wrenched herself around to face him. "I was not talking about Angelique," she snapped. "I'm not in the least offended at what she said, because every word of it's absolutely true. Crude, maybe, but I'll make allowances for that, since she got her cataracts ripped off without an anesthetic. But as for *you,* making me look like just another one of your bimbos in order to hold all the other ones off—''

''Can you think of a better way to discourage all the women who'd like to step into Angelique's shoes?'' He sounded perfectly calm.

''Yes. Rent a medevac helicopter and take off for Costa Rica!''

''Do be serious, Sabrina. As soon as they know there's a new woman in my life, they'll realize there's nothing to be gained by making spectacles of themselves, and they'll stop.''

''Or else they'll redouble their efforts. For all I know they'll lay siege to this house, and—''

''Not once they've seen you.'' He sounded very sure of himself. ''That's what makes you so perfect for this job, Sabrina. You're exactly the kind of woman I like.''

Sabrina almost screeched. ''You are a piece of work, Tanner! I ought to kick you in the kneecap for insulting me like that.''

He looked vaguely puzzled. ''What can you possibly find insulting about me saying that you're my kind of woman?''

''Make that your *other* kneecap!''

He shrugged. ''The point is, they'll take one look at you and they'll give up. I'm actually doing them a favor, saving them all the time they'd be wasting otherwise.''

Sabrina rolled her eyes heavenward.

''But you see, what they don't know is that because of certain characteristics you possess, I'm immune to you.''

''Now that's the first sensible thing you've said in some time,'' she muttered.

''And that's also the beauty of the whole idea. Not only

do you understand that I'm not vulnerable to you, but because of that little accident last night, you owe me. So, unlike every one of those women, you're under absolutely no illusion that you could crook your finger and ensnare me.''

The man was utterly serious and so completely sure of himself that he was mesmerizing. All Sabrina could do was stare at him in morbid fascination.

''You will very efficiently hold them off until I'm healthy enough to defend myself. Meanwhile, I'm in no danger from you. Once I'm back on my feet—'' he kissed his fingertips ''—it'll be goodbye, Sabrina.''

And he could start taking applications for bimbo of the week again, Sabrina thought. It couldn't happen quickly enough for her.

''It's perfect,'' Caleb said. ''Don't you agree?''

CHAPTER THREE

SABRINA stared at him with the same wariness that she would have accorded to a crocodile who'd suddenly reared his head from the middle of the threadbare carpet. She'd encountered egotistic males in her day, but never one quite as sure of himself as Caleb Tanner.

It was long past time for someone to teach the man a lesson, she thought. It would do him a great deal of good to be the jilted one for a change, chasing hungrily after a woman who ended up coldly rejecting him. Maybe even turning green around the edges with jealousy.

The woman who accomplished the feat would be striking a blow for her sisters around the world. In fact, Sabrina thought, she'd deserve sainthood.

For a moment, she actually considered trying it—and then her common sense reasserted itself. Not only weren't the odds of success exactly favorable, but she suspected that anyone who made the attempt to break Caleb Tanner's nonexistent heart was more likely to end up in a mental health ward than in the feminist hall of fame.

Even contemplating the idea was courting temporary insanity. She'd rather take on a suicide mission. *I'm immune to you,* he'd said—and Sabrina wouldn't put it past him to be telling the precise truth.

"Perfect?" she said. "Of course. Who could possibly question the clarity of your logic?"

Suspicion sparkled in Caleb's eyes, but before he could pursue the discussion the asthmatic doorbell chimed once more.

This time Caleb drew her down to sit facing him on the edge of the couch, with her hip nestled warmly against his. She landed a little off balance and had to brace a hand against the arm of the couch, just above his shoulder, to keep herself upright.

The man should be a stage director, she thought irritably. From the doorway, it would look as though they'd either just finished a kiss or were about to start one.

"Who's this visitor likely to be?" she asked. "I doubt the news of Angelique's comeuppance has spread across Denver in the ten minutes since she left. Is this likely to be one of her friends going behind her back in an attempt to seduce you, or someone from an entirely different branch of your feminine fan club?"

She heard the door squeak as Jennings opened it, and then a man's voice from the front hall made her release a long sigh of relief. "That's Jake," she said, and tried to sit up straighter.

Caleb's fingers curved around her wrist, preventing her from moving. "So?"

"There's no need to pretend for his sake. He wouldn't believe in this charade of yours, no matter what script you ran past him."

"Why not? Do you already have a boyfriend or something?"

"Oh, nobody you couldn't threaten into disappearing, I'm sure," Sabrina said dryly. "But that wasn't what I—"

"Then he'll believe it. He won't have any other choice."

"You mean you're going to lie to him."

"I mean we're both going to be very convincing. Let's get one thing straight, Sabrina. We aren't going to tell anybody about our private arrangement, and I mean *anybody*."

"But Jake's different," Sabrina argued. "He was right there yesterday. He heard what you said to me."

"And he will surely understand how profoundly I now regret that outburst," Caleb said.

His voice was deep and warm and so convincing that even Sabrina felt herself wavering. "How do you *do* that?" she asked admiringly. "If anybody ever does a remake of the Garden of Eden, you'd be a natural to play the serpent. One word from you and apple sales would skyrocket across the nation."

Caleb laid a finger across her mouth to shush her, then with the edge of his nail lightly traced the outline of her lips.

It was all she could do to sit still. From the corner of her eye, Sabrina noted that Jake had stopped on the threshold as if he'd run smack into a glass wall. Slowly, still watching the couple on the couch, he crossed the room and set a bulging briefcase on the floor next to the couch. "Don't think, just because you're wounded, that you're going to take a vacation, Caleb," he said. "I brought all the—"

Caleb didn't appear to hear. He was still looking soulfully into Sabrina's eyes.

"Caleb?" Jake said a little louder.

With a long sigh, Caleb let his fingertips drop from Sabrina's face—though he didn't release the wrist he was holding with his other hand—and turned toward Jake. "It's amazing how a simple accident can clarify your vision," he mused. "That fall yesterday was probably the luckiest thing that has ever happened to me, because I might never have met Sabrina otherwise."

Jake looked at him as if he were a scientific specimen. "Did they X ray your brain last night, Caleb?" he asked brusquely. "Because if not, they should have. Sorry, Sabrina, but—"

"Oh, you don't need to apologize to me, Jake." Sabrina

looked straight at Caleb while she peeled his fingers loose from her wrist. "I told you he'd never believe it."

"It may take him a little time to be convinced."

She stared at him in utter disbelief. Surely, in the face of Jake's obvious skepticism, Caleb wasn't going to pursue this nonsensical course. Was he?

He went on smoothly. "In fact, I expect lots of people are going to have their doubts for a while. Even though it isn't every day I confide that I'm serious about a woman, my friends may well be hesitant to believe—"

"You're absolutely right about that," Sabrina said judiciously. "It's not every day, and it's not exactly a whispered secret from you to your friends, either. From what I hear, it's more like twice a month and announced in the society page headlines."

Caleb's scowl was clearly a threat, but his voice was gentle and reasonable. "It's not at all the same thing, my dear. All the women who have been in my life up till now sort of run together into a blur as I think about them."

"*That* I can believe," Sabrina muttered unrepentantly.

"In fact, my darling, compared to you they don't even exist. I've never declared myself this way before, because I've never felt about any woman the way I feel about you, Sabrina."

The seemingly innocent sincerity in his voice left Sabrina staring at him in reluctant appreciation. She'd run into men before who had an endless supply of gall, and ones who possessed more than a touch of pure blarney. But she'd never before encountered a man who not only possessed both qualities but who used them so effectively. No wonder women fell over themselves to get near him—and no wonder he left such a swathe of destruction in his wake.

And to make it worse, he was telling the precise truth.

I've never felt about any woman the way I feel about you.
Well, two could play at that game.

She patted Caleb's cheek and said with utter honesty,
"And of course there's never been a man who could inspire
the sort of feelings I have for you, Caleb, dear."

She realized abruptly that it was the first time she'd actually said his name. She had neither anticipated nor
avoided the action; in fact, she hadn't given it any thought
at all. So it came as a shock to discover that the taste of
his name on her tongue was like the hottest of chili pep-
pers—it not only tingled at first exposure but it hinted of a
burn that instead of fading would grow even stronger with
time.

She edged away from him. "I'm sure you don't need me
sitting right here while you talk business."

"And you'd probably be bored by all the details," Caleb
agreed.

Sabrina bit her tongue to keep from retorting that she
wasn't his typical bimbo, incapable of understanding the
nuances of a business discussion. Bringing up the point
again would probably make no more impression on Caleb
than the last time she'd tried. Besides, it would just make
her situation worse by giving him an excuse to keep her
sitting beside him—the last place on earth she wanted to
be.

And what difference did it make, anyway, if he thought
she was as airheaded as the rest?

Talk about his ego, Sabrina told herself. *You've got more
than a little problem with your own, if you're worried about
what he thinks of you.*

She smiled sweetly and murmured, "And it would be so
rude of me to yawn in your face just because I couldn't
possibly keep up with the discussion, darling. Far better if

I just go away while you and Jake have your important talk.''

"But you won't go far." Caleb obviously wasn't asking a question, and under the statement lay a thread of steel that Sabrina had no trouble interpreting. *Don't even try running away*, he was reminding her.

As she stood up, Sabrina glanced at Jake and saw that his mouth was hanging open.

She wasn't surprised. A few minutes ago she'd expected him to see straight through the illusion—but that had been before she'd witnessed Caleb in full action. The man was a first-class magician.

If she, fully aware that this was only a performance, still found reality blurring around the edges, how could Jake possibly be expected to tell up from down?

Caleb watched her cross the room, and only when she was out of sight did he turn his attention to his visitor. Without thinking, he turned his body, too, and pain shot up his thigh and all the way down to his toes. "Damn that—" *woman*, he started to say, and changed it abruptly as he saw Jake's eyebrows start to rise "—doctor."

"For patching you back together?" Jake asked skeptically.

"For restricting my pain pills." Caleb shifted uneasily, trying to get the leg into a less uncomfortable position.

Jake's tone was dry. "Sure you haven't already taken way too many of them?"

"You think I must be drugged out of my mind," Caleb challenged, "just because I happened to notice that Sabrina is one beautiful woman."

She was, too, he reflected—in the same way a forest fire was beautiful. Of course, a wise man wouldn't let either one sneak up on him, surround him or get out of control....

"No argument about her looks, Caleb. I'd been wondering how long it would take you to spot her. But I've got a really uneasy feeling about this."

Caleb tried to shrug it off. "She's your fiancée's business partner, for heaven's sake."

"That's what makes me uneasy," Jake said. "I know her."

Caleb was certain he didn't want to hear the details, so he made a mental note to be cautious around Jake and changed the subject. "What's in that briefcase you brought?"

Jake shook his head and sighed, as if washing his hands of the discussion. "I gathered up everything you dropped in the lobby yesterday, plus some extra mail that arrived today."

Caleb glanced at the envelopes that poked out of the top of the briefcase. "That's quite a stack of job applications, considering it's only been a few weeks since we put the word out that we're looking for a CEO."

"I'm not surprised that people are jumping to apply. It's an intriguing assignment—nurturing a promising company like Tanner Electronics into a first-class position in the market."

Caleb grunted. "Are that many management experts out of work? And, if they don't have a job now, do we even want them?"

Jake grinned. "Some of them are between positions, but that doesn't mean they're incompetent. There's a guy in there who retired from the army, started a business, sold it for millions and is now looking for something to do with his free time. I wouldn't exactly call him unemployed. Then there are the ones who are working now but are looking for new challenges. And some of the most promising aren't really looking for work at all."

Caleb was flipping through papers. He looked up with a frown. "Then why are they sending us their résumés?"

"They're not. They may not even know about the job. There's a proposal there from a head-hunting firm, complete with a load of sample résumés. No names attached, of course—but if you like the looks of any of those people, the headhunters promise to deliver, even if they have to convince him or her to leave the current job."

Caleb whistled. "I don't suppose you'd like to take a guess as to what this person is likely to cost me."

"You don't want to turn your business over to someone who comes cheap but isn't any good. Sometimes the most expensive people are the real bargain because they get the job done."

"Maybe it's a good thing I still own most of the stock," Caleb muttered. "At least I won't have to explain to shareholders that their dividends are down because the new boss has a gold-plated desk."

"Or maybe you'll get really lucky and the only thing your new CEO wants is a par-three golf course built behind the factory."

"Not that I'll be playing anytime soon." Caleb looked down the length of the immobilizer with distaste.

"It's only November, Caleb. By the time golf season starts again, you'll be in great shape." Jake rose. "Look through those applications and see if any strike you as particularly interesting."

"I suppose you've already checked them out."

"I took a glance. I think there are a half dozen promising candidates—but I'd rather not give you my short list till you've had a chance to look them over yourself."

Caleb rubbed his knee and grumbled, half-seriously, "What you're really saying is that you don't trust my judgment where work's concerned any more than you do about women.''

Jake shook his head. ''It's a whole different thing. But take my advice and watch out for Sabrina. Don't underestimate her.''

Not a problem, Caleb told himself. *I already know exactly what the woman is capable of, and there's no chance in hell I'll forget it.*

His memory was in no danger of slipping a cog—not as long as his knee was aching as if it had been run over by a bulldozer.

He looked younger when he was asleep, Sabrina thought as she stood beside the couch with a water glass in one hand and a plastic pill cup in the other, looking at Caleb. Much younger, in fact.

Not that there wasn't a boyish quality about him at all times, she thought, but at the moment his air of innocence was a lot more believable than it was when his calculator of a brain was operating full tilt. He'd turned his head till his cheek was nestled into the pillow, and his lashes, incredibly long, dark and curly, lay heavily across cheeks touched by dark stubble and flushed by sleep—or fever.

She frowned, set down the pill cup and tried to very gently lay the back of her free hand against his forehead to check his temperature.

He jerked away, and his elbow bumped her arm, sending the water glass spinning. Almost as if it were weightless, it seemed to hover above him, pitching and yawing like a space capsule as it sent spurts of cold water onto his face, his hair, his sweatshirt.

The glass fell on his chest, and an ice cube bounced out and slid squarely down the side of his neck.

Sabrina bit her lip. She was doomed.

"What do you think you're doing?" Caleb sputtered. He scrambled to get hold of the errant ice cube.

"I was trying to check you for fever."

"And so as not to waste a moment, giving me a cold bath at the same time!"

"You're the one who knocked the glass out of my hand," Sabrina pointed out.

"You should know better than to wake me up like that."

"I wasn't trying to wake you. Are you always such a touchy sleeper? One would think you have a guilty conscience—or that you make a habit of defending yourself the moment you wake up."

"I'm not touchy," he growled. "Your hands are still cold from putting ice packs on my knee. I don't know how you'd expect to recognize fever when your hands are—"

"The last ice pack I brought in was half an hour ago. It's actually time to take it off."

"Really? How time flies when you're having fun."

"And you can have another pain pill, as soon as I get some more water so you can take it." She reached for the glass, still balanced on his chest.

"Do me a favor—don't move." He swirled the last remaining liquid in the glass and popped the tablet in his mouth. "There's enough here."

"That's not good for you, swallowing pills almost dry. I'll get you another—"

"Thanks, but I'd rather not risk it. I'll wring the excess out of my sweatshirt and drink that." He flung his head back against the arm of the couch and closed his eyes. "What time is it?"

"A little past two."

He groaned. "This day has been at least three months long."

Sabrina's conscience twinged. "Can I do anything for you?"

"Yeah. It's too quiet in here."

She put out a hand, palm up. "Have credit card, will shop," she offered.

He looked at her warily through half-open eyes. "For what?"

"For a decent sound system for this room. I'll get you a bargain, too. Shopping is one of the things I do best. My partners often turn those jobs over to me."

"And it would get you out of here for a while."

"That had occurred to me," she admitted.

"Well, you're not going. Sit down and entertain me."

"With what? I played the flute when I was a kid, but I'm afraid I don't have one on me at the moment. Cassie's the expert at poetry reading, Paige is a much better singer than I—"

"Talk to me. Tell me why, for instance, I was fortunate enough not to ever meet you before yesterday."

Sabrina bit her tongue to keep from retorting, and said reasonably, "Well, it has only been a matter of weeks since you decided to let Rent-A-Wife supply perks and services to your employees to keep them happy."

"And your partners were keeping you away from the office, right?"

"You mean, so I wouldn't blow the place up? Not at all. I've spent as much time at Tanner as Cassie and Paige have. In fact, we've been taking turns, each spending at least a day every week taking care of the errands and requests. Either you haven't put your name on the list at all, or it's been either Paige or Cassie on duty when you asked for something."

"Till yesterday when my luck ran out altogether," he mused. "Tell me about the errands and requests."

"You mean what your employees are asking for? Mostly the same stuff the rest of our clients want. Delivering the car for an oil change, dropping off last season's clothes to the resale shop, taking the dog to the vet for his shots, picking up tickets at the box office. The kind of thing everybody needs done, but nobody has time to actually keep up with."

"And people pay you to do that sort of thing?"

"You pay Jennings, don't you? I'm sure he takes care of your errand running and dry-cleaning and things of that sort. The truly rich—like you—have personal assistants. But what does the rest of the population do when they need help?"

Caleb said obediently, "They rent a wife."

"You're a quick study. *Every working person needs a wife*—that's our motto. Of course, as the business grows, I find myself wishing that we'd called it something different. Maybe we should have focused on the image of a concierge, like the big hotels have to take care of their guests, rather than making it sound so domestic."

"The name does leave the door open for misunderstandings," Caleb said. His tone was almost solemn, but the sparkle in his eyes said he was quite willing to expand on the theme. "When I first heard about it, I thought—"

"Anyway," Sabrina said hastily, "whatever the name, I've never regretted joining in this venture. Paige and Cassie are my good friends as well as good partners."

"There's a feminine viewpoint for you. Thinking you have to like somebody to do business with them."

"Oh, I wouldn't go so far as to say I insist on it. Take you, for instance—"

"Me? Oh, you mean you don't like me."

"A perceptive soul, aren't you, Caleb?"

"Why don't you fancy me? I'm likable."

"And I'll bet you can give me testimonials to that effect from at least a hundred women. Though if I were you," she added thoughtfully, "I don't think I'd ask Angelique for a reference any time soon."

She was getting so used to the doorbell that she could identify the first telltale click before it started to wheeze. So could Caleb, obviously; the doorbell had barely begun to gasp when he beckoned her toward the couch.

Sabrina shook her head and stayed in her chair.

"You're not being very cooperative," he said. "After all, I'm the one who's taking the risk by inviting you over here. It might not be just water next time. For all I know, you've got a fountain pen in your pocket and if I so much as brush against you I'll get a squirt of black ink in the eyes."

As the front door creaked open, Sabrina put her finger across her lips.

They listened as Jennings greeted a guest who was obviously feminine and obviously disappointed at the news she was hearing. Then the door closed, and Jennings's steps retreated toward the back of the house. Silence descended.

Sabrina felt like patting herself on the back. She met Caleb's questioning gaze and said proudly, "I instructed Jennings to tell everybody you were asleep. It's a simple, classic justification for refusing a guest, and nobody can argue with it. And it proves, by the way, that he's perfectly capable of defending you all by himself."

"I can't be asleep for the entire next week."

"So I'll give him a few more ready-made excuses, and he can use them in rotation. All he needs is a little guidance, you know, and some encouragement to stand up for himself. You really don't need me as a bodyguard after all." She settled into her chair with an air of satisfaction. "And you won't have to worry about fountain pens or—"

Caleb wasn't looking at her any more. He was staring over her shoulder at the French door behind her. "Oh, really?" he said dryly.

Curious, Sabrina had started to turn toward the door when she heard a frantic tapping on the glass and the same feminine voice, somewhat muffled, say, "Caleb! You *are* awake!"

Outside the door stood a tiny brunette in a short, tight electric-blue dress that would have looked more at home in the red-light district. The way she was bending forward to peer through the glass had almost caused her to spill out of her low cut neckline.

Sabrina sighed. "Want me to let her in?"

"Might as well. If I know Muffy, she's not going to give up. And I can hardly pretend that I've gone to sleep this very instant."

The brunette cast one curious glance at Sabrina before she darted across the room and flung herself down beside Caleb. He winced as the couch cushions bounced under her weight and glared at Sabrina as if to say, *See? I know what I'm talking about. And this is all your fault.*

Obviously, Sabrina thought, she had underestimated the competition. It hadn't occurred to her that Caleb's women might descend to creeping through the bushes to window peek.

She spread her hands in a gesture of helpless apology and sat on the edge of her chair again.

Muffy had started to babble. "I just knew your man had to be wrong, Caleb. You wouldn't be asleep in the middle of the day, a big strong man like you. Though I simply can't believe what I'm seeing, you poor darling! Such a terrible thing to happen, having to be caged up this way. You'll have to be very careful not to lose your strength as you lie around waiting to heal. But I've brought you the very best medicine for this kind of injury.''

Caleb showed a spark of interest. "Napoleon brandy?" he asked with a hopeful note in his voice.

Muffy giggled. "Of course not. My aromatherapist made these up just for you." She opened her handbag and pulled out a half dozen small glass flasks. She set them in a row on the coffee table, then tugged the cork from the mouth of the largest one and waved it under Caleb's nose. "Be sure you sniff one of these every hour, for at least a minute each time, and you'll have no more problem with feeling weak." She folded his hand around the flask.

"Just light-headed," he muttered.

Caleb's eyes were watering, Sabrina noted, and he looked as if he was trying not to choke. She got up and took the flask from him.

Muffy didn't seem to notice. "It is such a shame, having you laid up like this just as skiing season is starting and everything." She leaned closer to him. "And you were going to teach me your slalom techniques this winter."

"Was I?" Caleb asked absently. "I hadn't even gotten around to thinking about skiing." His voice dripped sadness. "But you're right, Muffy. That's going to be out, probably for the whole season." He didn't look at Sabrina. He didn't have to; the message was clear.

She wanted to growl. No, she wanted to yank Muffy off the couch by the hair and throw her outside, straight into the thorniest bush she could find. Didn't she have enough trouble already without people coming around to remind Caleb of everything he was going to miss—and incidentally giving him one more thing to blame Sabrina for?

And as for Caleb, Sabrina thought irritably, what about a speck of gratitude toward her for relieving him of a bottle of liquid that smelled vaguely like a gym locker that hadn't felt a breath of fresh air in years?

Muffy giggled. "Of course, you could always just stay in the lodge. I'd be happy to keep you entertained while everyone else is on the slopes." Her breathy little voice made it quite clear what she was offering.

Sabrina rolled her eyes skyward. "It's very selfless of you to make such a generous offer," she said, "but keeping Caleb entertained is my department now."

Muffy turned to stare at her. "And who do you think you are?"

"The woman he's asked to be with him while he recovers," Sabrina said firmly. "Which you aren't. Thanks very much for stopping by, but it's time for you to go."

She walked Muffy to the door and returned, dusting off her hands. "I feel like a bouncer."

Caleb sneezed. "Get rid of that smelly stuff, will you?"

Sabrina gathered up the flasks, noting that at least one of them was cut crystal. "Do you know what she probably paid for all this?"

"How much do you think she dropped at the scratch and sniff store?"

Sabrina counted flasks and gave him her estimate. "Though on the other hand, she may have used a budget aromatherapist, because a good one would have made sure the smell didn't knock you over like that."

"What a waste," Caleb groaned. "For that much money she could have got me the passenger car I want."

"Passenger car? I thought you were such a fiend on motorcycles you wouldn't own a car."

"For my railroad."

"You *own* a—never mind." Sabrina cast a critical glance around the room. "You really should consider the benefit of curtains, at least. I can't be in the room with you every minute.''

"Why not?"

"Because you're not paying me enough.''

"I'm not paying you anything.''

"Precisely. Of course, no amount of money would be enough—but that's another line of discussion altogether. I find it hard to believe that out of all your female friends, not even one of them has tried to renovate this house. Or were they smart enough to know that you'd see the offer as a ploy for permanence?''

"I've only lived here a few weeks.''

"I know. Jennings told me. Still, if it didn't take me more than three minutes to mentally redesign this room—''

"Don't get that gleam in your eyes, Sabrina.''

"And don't you imagine things. I said I can visualize what it could be like; I didn't offer to make it happen. Why should I take on the job and give you something else not to pay me for?''

"You know,'' Caleb said thoughtfully, "you may have a point, at that.''

She was momentarily baffled. "What are you talking about?''

"Someday I will have to let somebody redecorate. And whoever does the work, even if it's a professional, is likely to get ideas about eternity.''

"You really do think you're irresistible, don't you?'' *But why wouldn't he?* asked a little voice in the back of her brain. *He's a pretty classy package, after all.* "Hire a man,'' she advised.

Caleb considered the suggestion and shrugged. "Not a bad idea, but it would be even more sensible of me to let you tackle the job instead.''

"I just told you—''

"You can deal with the decorators and protect me from them at the same time."

"In case you've forgotten," Sabrina said firmly, "I didn't volunteer."

"It'll be a far more efficient use of your time when I'm trying to catch up on my work if you're looking at samples and paint chips rather than just wandering around the house."

"I'd happily wander around the city instead, doing my real job."

"That's not an option. Just because I'm busy doesn't mean I won't want something on a moment's notice. No, this is the perfect idea."

"And the perfect revenge for my mistake in letting Muffy get past the barricades—right?"

He grinned. "You're almost as perceptive as I am, Sabrina. Just remember—no ruffles. And nothing purple."

He leaned back and closed his eyes once more. After a moment he asked, "No more arguments?"

"Obviously," Sabrina said gently, "there's no point in trying to change your mind." She would just ignore him instead, she decided. If she put off doing anything about this brainstorm of his, within a few days—by the time he was back on his feet—he'd no doubt have forgotten the whole idea. Or else he'd be looking forward to getting to know a dozen or so eager decorators....

"Good," he said lazily. "I'm glad you've come to such a sensible conclusion."

Within a few minutes he'd drifted off to sleep again. Sabrina waited till his breathing was deep and even, and then she picked up all the aromatherapy supplies and carried them upstairs. She suspected he'd meant for her to throw the flasks away, but her sense of self-preservation suggested that she put them in a closet somewhere instead, in case he changed his mind.

All the doors stood open, and so Sabrina couldn't help noticing that the upper level of the house was almost as bleak and neglected as the living room. Every wall was dingy or stained. Of the three main bedrooms, one was completely empty, one held a king-size waterbed and nothing else, and one had a blown-up air mattress in the middle of the floor. She was stashing the flasks on a shelf in the empty room when the front door creaked.

Had she missed the bell, or had someone just wandered in off the street? It probably didn't matter; the important thing was to make sure the caller was sent firmly away. The last thing Sabrina needed was another Muffy getting to Caleb and causing trouble.

From the head of the stairs she couldn't see the caller, only the half-open door, but she was relieved to see that Jennings was on the job. With one hand on the knob, he appeared to be holding back whoever stood outside.

But Sabrina's relief was short-lived, for instead of using the excuse she'd given him—which in this case even had the benefit of being absolutely true—Jennings stepped back from the door in an obvious invitation, and a woman's voice said very clearly, "Thank you, Jennings."

Severe countermeasures were indicated, Sabrina thought.

She bounded down the steps. "Jennings," she said with all the breathless imperiousness she could muster. "I'm certain you aren't going against Caleb's instructions to obey my orders, so that must mean you simply didn't understand. I really must insist that no one be allowed to disturb—"

From behind the door emerged one of the most beautiful women Sabrina had ever seen. She was tall and slim, dressed in a black suit that had obviously come from the hand of a master designer. Her enormous midnight blue eyes and a blaze of silver hair almost made the delicate lines in her face disappear.

"Even his mother?" the woman asked gently, and held out a hand. "I'm Catherine Tanner. And you?"

CHAPTER FOUR

SABRINA'S knees threatened to give way, and she clung to the banister till her fingers cramped, willing herself not to fall down the stairs. Though, she thought fleetingly, if she *did* go headlong and break her neck, at least she wouldn't have to answer Catherine Tanner's question.

And you? What was she supposed to say to that?

The cover story? True, Caleb had declared that they weren't going to take anyone into total confidence—but he'd been talking about an employee right then, not his mother, for heaven's sake. Surely he didn't intend to lie to her.

The truth, then?

"I'm..." she began. "I'm Caleb's...."

"That much," Catherine Tanner said dryly, "is apparent."

Isn't that just great, Sabrina thought. She was off the hook—for the moment at least, though probably not completely—but it was at the cost of looking like the sort of woman who couldn't construct a full sentence without assistance. At this rate, she told herself irritably, within a week she wouldn't have to practice at acting like an airhead, it would come quite naturally.

Briskly, Catherine said, "I'd love a cup of your coffee, Jennings. If you'd care to join me, Miss—"

Reluctantly, Sabrina descended to the hallway. As Catherine turned toward the living room, Sabrina put out a hand to stop her. "He really is asleep," she said.

"Yes, Jennings told me. The fact that he's managing to

snooze on that ghastly, uncomfortable couch is what surprises me." Catherine eyed the hospital bed, still as pristine as the moment it had been set up, in the dining room. Then she tiptoed past the door and led the way into the sunny family room at the back of the house. "In fact, there's only one chair in this entire house that's fit to sit on, and I'm going to invoke the privilege of age and claim it."

"Be my guest," Sabrina said. "I mean—not really *my* guest, of course, but—"

Catherine waved a dismissing hand. "I hope you won't be offended if I point out that I've met far too many of my son's women friends to be embarrassed by the situation in which we find ourselves. Of course, if you're sensitive about it—"

"Not at all," Sabrina said faintly.

"Good. If you were, I'd suggest that you run as far and as fast as possible from Caleb before you encounter the inevitable disillusionment."

I wish I could run, Sabrina thought.

"You look a bit taken aback by the fact that unlike many mothers I don't see my son as ultimate perfection," Catherine observed.

Jennings came in, silent-footed, carrying a silver tray, and poured their coffee into a pair of bone china mugs. Catherine lifted her cup and smiled at Jennings. "I've always liked these cups, that's why I bought them for Caleb's kitchen. Thank you for remembering."

Sabrina, grateful for the interruption that meant she didn't have to answer the last comment, folded her hands around the warm china. "Caleb had a pain pill just a few minutes ago. I'll write down the full schedule for you, of what he needs to take and when—"

"Why?" Catherine asked crisply.

Sabrina was puzzled. "Because you'll need to know. I'm sure now that you're here—"

"I stopped in to see how he was doing, not to play nurse-maid."

From the living room, Caleb called, "Sabrina! Where are you?"

Catherine's eyebrows rose. "My goodness. He hasn't sounded that pathetically weak and helpless since he was seven years old and had chicken pox."

Sabrina set her cup onto the tray and hastily headed for the living room.

"Are you quite sure you want to get in the habit of jumping like this when he calls?" Catherine asked politely. "His ego is quite large enough as it is, you know, without being waited on."

Sabrina didn't pause. *You'll get no argument from me on that subject,* she thought. But at the moment she'd rather look like a lovestruck fool than miss a chance to warn Caleb of his visitor before he said something he'd regret— or blame her for.

"Look who's dropped in to see how you're doing after your accident," she said as she rounded the corner.

Caleb scowled at the warning note in her voice. "I thought we'd agreed— Oh, hello, Mom. How'd you hear about this?"

Unhurried, with her coffee cup in her hand, Catherine crossed the room to stand over him. "How do I always hear what you're up to?" she said cryptically. "I came into town to attend a charity reception tonight, so I thought I'd drop in to see how you're doing. Miserably, I see."

He tried to push himself into a sitting position, and Sabrina jumped to help. "It's not as bad as it could be," he said. "Having Sabrina beside me makes all the difference in the world."

"I'm sure it does," Catherine said dryly. "Lucky girl. Regrettably, I can't stay just now to get to know her better. Now that I see how well cared for you are, Caleb, I need to be going, or I'll be late for the reception. But I'll try to stop again tomorrow before I go home."

"You're not staying here?" Sabrina felt her last hope for an early escape vanish.

"My dear." Catherine's voice was drenched with incredulity. "You *are* joking."

"My mother won't stay in this den of iniquity."

"I never told you that, Caleb. I said I wouldn't stay in a tenement."

Sabrina couldn't blame her. "Guest room" was an overly polite term when the best amenity the place offered was an air mattress on the floor.

"Sabrina's going to start redecorating," Caleb said casually. "Right away, in fact."

Catherine's eyes narrowed, and the look she gave Sabrina was filled with surprise with a generous sprinkling of respect. "That's a first," she said under her breath.

Obviously, Sabrina thought, *I've come up a couple of steps in the lady's estimation.*

When she saw Catherine to the door a few minutes later, however, the older woman murmured, "Redecorating, hmm? I congratulate you. Still, I'd advise that you don't start needlepointing seat covers for a dozen dining room chairs."

Sabrina bit her tongue to keep from saying that in her estimation this partnership wasn't likely to last as long as it took paint to dry, and she settled for a vague smile instead.

She probably looked like a first-class bimbo with that fatuous smile on her face, she thought. And she felt like a fool. Acting as if she didn't even have the sense to know when she was being warned...

But of course it didn't matter what Catherine Tanner thought of her. It certainly wasn't the fact that it was Caleb's mother who was issuing admonitions that was the problem. Sabrina would have been every bit as sensitive had anyone else thought she was actually naive enough to believe she might be the woman to stop Caleb Tanner's wanderings.

Wouldn't she?

Not quite, she admitted. This was different somehow.

For one thing, she told herself, nobody else had much right to an opinion, while Catherine Tanner had a personal stake in the matter. Other observers of this circus act might raise eyebrows or gossip or even laugh. But if anyone was likely to fret or brood, it would be Caleb's mother. And despite Catherine's half cynical reaction, this stunt had to be bothering her.

That, Sabrina decided, must be why she was feeling especially jittery. Not that she could do anything to modify Catherine's reaction, of course.

She waved from the doorway as Catherine got into her Mercedes, and when she returned to the living room, Caleb looked almost gleeful. "That went well."

"Not necessarily."

"The redecorating thing was an inspiration." He paused and inspected her closely. "You don't agree, do you? In fact, you sound like the voice of doom. Don't you think we convinced my mother?"

"I think all you managed to do was upset her."

Caleb looked thoughtful. "Then we'll just have to try harder."

"I don't suppose you'd consider just being truthful instead? There's something really distasteful about deliberately trying to send your mother gaga over a woman you aren't even serious about."

"My mother is too sensible to go gaga over anything."

"Too sensible? Or just too experienced with your behavior?" She gave up the idea of making a dent in his self-assurance. "Nevertheless, I think you should be prepared for tougher questions tomorrow, after she's had a chance to think this through."

He looked thoughtful. "Not a bad idea. Tell Jennings to order in dinner tonight from the Pinnacle—"

"Why am I not surprised that Denver's best restaurant does take-out? At least for certain clients?"

"And then you can tell me everything I need to know." Sabrina frowned. "About what?"

"You, of course. What's the matter? It was your idea for me to do my homework so I'd be ready for Mom tomorrow. I'll need to know things like where you grew up, and what your comfort foods are, and how you like your coffee, and who your first boyfriend was, and—"

"I didn't exactly mean you should study for an exam with me as the subject. Who in their right minds would expect you to know what I eat when I'm unhappy?"

"Now that you mention it," Caleb said, "it doesn't sound like a very likely piece of knowledge. The only way I'd have that information at my fingertips is if I've already made you unhappy—not the image we're trying to create—or if I'm intending to disappoint you. When the real truth is—"

"The truth is, you don't care a bit. If I told you I eat live crickets when I'm miserable, you wouldn't even blink. How much did you really know about Angelique, anyway?"

"That's different."

"It certainly is."

"*She* may have been trying to make people think that she was more than a passing interest, but *I* never did."

"I'm honored at the distinction," Sabrina said dryly. "But that brings us back to my point. I think you should consider what you're trying to accomplish here. Your mother might actually be a better ally if she knew exactly what was going on instead of feeling skeptical about the whole thing."

"You really think she'd cooperate?"

"How should I know? She's your mother, not mine." *And two women who are less alike than Catherine Tanner and Geneva Saunders would be hard to find*, Sabrina thought. "But I don't imagine for a minute that you're going to convince her beyond a shadow of doubt, so unless you want her going around acting dubious about our supposed romance—"

"You believe I should tell her the truth." Caleb frowned. "I'll think about it. In the meantime, though—just in case—tell me what I need to know to pass a test on Sabrina Saunders. Who *was* your first boyfriend?"

Sabrina never did answer the question. Getting information out of her, Caleb concluded, was something like acquiring top secrets from a case-hardened spy. He'd never encountered a woman so reluctant to talk about herself.

By the time they'd finished the Pinnacle's excellent prime rib, she had admitted to being raised in Colorado Springs, and he'd observed that she drank decaf with sweetener, no cream. But that was just about the sum of his knowledge.

He found himself yawning over the chocolate cheesecake, and he didn't protest when Sabrina took his coffee cup out of his hand before he'd finished with it.

"It's your bedtime," she said firmly. "Right now, so don't give me any argument about it."

Caleb tried to smother another yawn. "I love it when you talk dirty, Sabrina. Do you like leather and whips, too? I've been invited into bed before, of course—"

Her eyes went wide with mock astonishment. "You're joking. Really? You have?"

"But I don't think I've ever before been ordered."

She stood up and reached for his crutches. "Not since you were seven and had chicken pox, at any rate."

"Now that's not fair," he complained. "You've obviously done your research on me, but you won't tell me anything about you. Do I have to put a private detective on the case?"

"Don't bother. By the time he figures out there's no mystery, your knee will have healed and I'll be out of here."

There was no doubt about the eagerness in her tone. Well, it couldn't happen too quickly for him, either, Caleb thought. He was feeling so anxious he was twitchy underneath the exhaustion. Though why he should be feeling tired when all he'd done all day was to lie on the couch, spar with Sabrina and read a few job applications was beyond him.

"Give Jennings a call, will you?" He caught the glimmer of relief in her eyes and went on with a hint of malice, "Not to help me into bed, because that's your job. But he can bring down the air mattress for you."

"How perfectly comfy that sounds."

"If you're suggesting crawling in with me instead—"

"I'd rather sleep on a bed of embers, thank you."

"Then don't gripe about the air mattress." He looked her over. "Oh, and have him dig up something for you to

sleep in. I must have some pajamas around here somewhere.''

"Still in the original Christmas box, no doubt," Sabrina
muttered.

"Probably," Caleb said agreeably.

"I'm amazed at anyone being wasteful enough to buy
you such a thing. Surely even the dimmest of your girlfriends didn't expect you to *use*... Never mind."

He grinned. She had turned a delightful shade of shell
pink.

"Anyway," she went on, her voice sounding determined, "Jennings doesn't need to turn out the attic at this
hour in search of pajamas."

"Because you sleep in the nude," Caleb speculated.

"Why not?" she said sweetly. "It wouldn't matter anyway, because you're immune to me. Remember?"

"Oh, yes. It'll be an interesting test, though."

"Don't get your hopes up. As a matter of fact, I *don't*
sleep in the nude. I had a nightgown in my car."

Caleb felt his eyebrows soar. "My goodness," he
drawled. "You're an unexpectedly well-prepared young
woman."

She wasn't just pink anymore, he noted; there were hec-
tic red patches in her cheeks, and her eyes sparkled with
irritation. "Only because I happened to buy it just yesterday, and in all the fuss of the party and the accident last
night, I forgot to take the bags out of the car when I finally
got home."

"Of course," he said gently. "You don't owe me an
explanation, Sabrina. And in any case, I already knew that
you don't leave a nightie in your car because you're in the
habit of sleepovers."

"Thanks for that much, at least."

If it hadn't been for the grudging note in her voice, he

might have left it at that—but the opportunity was too good to miss. "If you made a regular thing of staying with a man, Sabrina, you wouldn't bother with nightgowns any more than I do with pajamas."

She stuck her tongue out at him.

Caleb grinned at the childish display—he'd asked for it, that was sure—and swung himself up on his crutches. He was feeling a little light-headed, he noted. In addition, despite the fact that it was mostly canvas, the immobilizer felt heavy as well as awkward, and it took a bit of time and effort to get his balance.

Just getting from the living room across the wide hallway to the hospital bed left him feeling as if he'd fought a major battle. He made his way around the air mattress that Jennings had already put in place, sank gratefully onto the side of the bed and let Sabrina strip off the sweatshirt he'd been wearing all day. As he stretched out, the sheets felt pleasantly cool against his skin.

"The whole business about the nightgown reminds me of something, though," she said.

Caleb closed his eyes. "Don't tell me, let me speculate. Maybe I can even take my mind off this damned knee and put myself to sleep by fantasizing what a nightgown might remind you of."

"Probably not the same thing it brings to your mind, so you may as well not bother to guess. It's going to be a problem, too. The reason I was in the store in the first place was to buy a gift for Cassie's bridal shower."

"Shower," Caleb murmured. "You don't know how good that sounds."

"Are you always so easily distracted?"

"Only when I'm taking pain pills by the barrel. Do you suppose if I was careful to put my weight on my one good leg I could stand in the shower... No, I probably couldn't keep my balance for nearly long enough. Of course, you *could* climb in with me and—"

Sabrina raised her voice. "As I was saying, I was buying a gift for Cassie's bridal shower, which is going to be held on Saturday evening. And since I'm not only her business partner but one of the hostesses, *and* since the party's being held at my condo, I'm going to have to be there."

"No problem."

She looked at him warily. "You mean I can go home? Just like that? What happened to holding me hostage?"

Caleb shrugged. "I'll go with you. By Saturday I should be up and around a bit, and appearing together at an event like that will be a real statement of how much we mean to each other. The fact that you won't leave me alone even for a few hours…"

"You can't come."

"Why not? I thought my mother said once that showers aren't usually the sort of event where an extra warm body would ruin the catering."

"It's not that." She sounded reluctant to admit it. "It's just that you'll probably be the only man there."

"I can handle it."

"Foolish me," she muttered, "to think something like that might bother you."

Caleb sank back against the raised head of the bed. His head had started swimming with exhaustion. "If you'd prop one of those pillows under my knee, Sabrina…"

She adjusted the pillow and turned off the lights, leaving only the glow of the dimmed hallway chandelier to provide illumination, and went off to change into her nightgown. By the time she came back Caleb's head had stopped spinning.

Quiet as she was, he heard her footsteps and said drowsily, "Answer a question for me, or I'm apt to have nightmares about crickets. What do you really like to eat when you're sad?''

"You don't give up, do you, Tanner?''

"Not easily.''

She sighed. "Turtles.''

"You mean those sticky caramel, chocolate and pecan things?''

"No,'' she said gently. "I mean the big ones at the zoo, shells and all.''

He turned his head to smile at her, and thought for an instant that he was hallucinating. He blinked and looked again. No, she really was standing just inside the doorway, wearing an oversize, man-tailored emerald-green satin nightshirt, which she probably believed was all-concealing. In full light, it might have been—but the glow from the hallway, though it was barely strong enough to throw shadows, somehow turned her body into a living sculpture and made the satin seem to disappear altogether.

Stunned by the sight, Caleb sucked in a deep, involuntary breath. She moved quickly to his side to lay a hand on his forehead. "You're hurting, aren't you? What can I do?''

He shook his head, but he was lying, for he was in pain— though this time his knee had nothing to do with it.

And he didn't think she wanted to hear his suggestions of what she could do to relieve his discomfort.

He'd said he was immune to her, and despite the way he was feeling at the moment, he'd stand by that declaration. So what if he'd caught a glimpse of an incredible body, and his own had reacted quite predictably? All it proved was that his hormones were still in perfectly good working order. It didn't mean that he'd forgotten the woman was a hazard or that he was in any danger of taking her seriously.

Anyway, he'd said he was immune. He'd never claimed to be dead.

Sabrina was still asleep when something started buzzing on the floor next to her air mattress. It took two cycles before she could identify the sound as the telephone she'd plugged in last night, and another to roll over and get her hand on it. Her eyes were still half closed as she lifted the receiver to her ear.

"Sabrina?" Jake said. "Sorry, I didn't think before I called, but it is after nine o'clock. I didn't expect to wake you."

"It's okay," she mumbled. "Caleb had a pretty restless night, and so every time he moved I roused up, too." She didn't even consider what she was saying till the words were out, and as the implication hit her, her eyes snapped wide open. "I mean— At least, I *don't* mean that I—"

From the hospital bed, Caleb gave a snort of laughter. "That's the way, Sabrina," he said softly. "Keep that up and I won't have to even try to convince anybody."

Jake said, "If it's okay with you, Sabrina, I'd just as soon not hear the details."

Sabrina made a face at Caleb and said, "I didn't think you were a prude, Jake. Just because it sounds like we spent the night in the same bed doesn't mean we did."

"Whatever you say, Sabrina." Jake sounded less than convinced. "Can I talk to Caleb?"

She passed the phone up and sank onto the air mattress, her arm flung over her eyes. *Great move,* she told herself. *And you're not even out of bed yet.*

"Just because it sounds like we spent the night in the same bed doesn't mean we didn't, either," Caleb said cheerfully. "What can I do for you this morning, Jake?"

Sabrina picked up a pillow, thought about laying it across

Caleb's face and pushing down hard, and settled for throwing it at him before she walked out.

She took her time in the shower; the upstairs bathroom was enormous and old-fashioned, and because the previous owners of the house had obviously never heard of water-saving devices, the shower was the most luxurious she'd experienced in years. By the time she came downstairs again, dressed once more in yesterday's suit, Caleb was sitting on the edge of his bed.

He looked better, Sabrina thought; his color had returned. With any luck, he'd decide he didn't need her any more at all.

"Where did you disappear to?" he demanded.

"If I told you, it would only make you unhappy," she pointed out. "But let me just say that I know now why you bought the house. It's because you got tired of the stingy plumbing they put in apartments, right?"

He didn't rise to the bait as she'd expected. "Jake wasn't calling just to be sociable," he said. "I have to go into the office today."

"Why?"

"Because I am still running a company, and I can't be out for days on end."

"One day," she corrected. "You stayed home for one day. It's hardly like you deserted the place."

"And also because there's a man coming in to meet with me."

"A very important man, obviously, if you're going to all the trouble. Couldn't he come here instead of dragging you out?"

"Here?"

Sabrina took her first good look at the dining room in daylight and realized that it made the rest of the house look good; the walls were dingy beige and spotted with what looked like mildew. "On second thought," she added, "forget I asked that question. In its present state, this house hardly projects the sort of image you want. But surely this could wait till you're back on your feet. Another day or two—"

"It's Friday," Caleb reminded her. "And he'll only be in town today." He reached for his crutches. "Jennings! Bring me some clothes, will you?"

By the time he was dressed, he was looking pale once more, and Sabrina thought it was only his pride that made him persist. With some difficulty, he negotiated the crumbling patio to stand beside her small convertible. "I won't fit," he said.

"We could call a cab."

"That would take too long. You know, it would help if it was the other leg. Then I might be able to sit down and sort of twist my way in."

"If you're suggesting that I damage it, too, so you'll have a matched set—" Caleb scowled, and Sabrina decided to stop while she was ahead. "We could always put the top down and hang your leg out over the side."

"And give me pneumonia. You said something once about your job being like a concierge's."

"Yeah. Why?"

"Because I've just come up with a new name for your business. Concierge in a Can. As in tin can—like this car."

Sabrina bristled. "I'll have you know this is a vintage car. My grandfather bought it for me when I got my driver's license."

She saw the sudden sparkle in his eyes and realized she'd inadvertently given up another tidbit of information.

"And that was how long ago?" he asked casually.

"Well, I'm not ready to retire just yet. And you have a

nerve to talk about my car, when the only means of transportation you own is a motorcycle.''

"It's no ordinary motorcycle. Maybe when I'm healed
up I'll take you for a spin. On the other hand,'' he added
thoughtfully, ''I wouldn't like to end up under the front
end of a Mack truck, and with you along—''

"With your high opinion of me, I'm amazed you'll let
me drive.''

"If I had any real choice, I wouldn't.'' He managed to
insert himself into the passenger bucket seat, but only by
letting his injured leg sprawl across the driver's space.

Sabrina looked at the arrangement doubtfully. ''Are you
absolutely certain you don't want me to call a limo service?''

"That would be a waste of all the energy I spent getting
in here.''

"Where am I supposed to sit?'' Sabrina asked.

With both hands on his knee, Caleb lifted his leg enough
for her to slide into place.

She looked thoughtfully at his leg, stretched across her
lap. ''One thing about it,'' she said. ''I don't much need a
seat belt with this barricade in the way. And you're wrin-
kling my suit, after Jennings went to such trouble to press
it.''

"So have him press it again.''

"And what am I supposed to wear while he's doing the
job? When I've dropped you off at the office I'm going
home to pick up some clothes and check on—''

Caleb shook his head. ''I'll need help while I'm there,
too.''

"There are a hundred people in that office building who
could give you a hand.''

"None of them understand my situation the way you do,

darling. And of course not everyone can be trusted to keep the things they hear confidential.''

''You want me standing beside you during your meeting, too?''

''Maybe not standing beside me, but definitely within earshot.''

''Ready to jump to attention. What are you trying to do, impress this very important person? What makes him so very important, anyway?''

''He's a headhunter.''

''Oh.''

Caleb grinned. ''Not the kind who wears war paint and feathers and skins and carries a spear. He's proposing a plan to find the new CEO I'm looking for.''

''I know what a headhunter is.'' *And your imagination is running wild,* she told herself. ''Why do you need a headhunter, anyway?''

''Because not just anyone will do for this position.''

''Why not? You did the job just fine for years, didn't you? Why are you giving it up, anyway?''

''To have more time for you, my dear.'' He sounded like Little Red Riding Hood's wolf.

Even though she knew he was joking, Sabrina couldn't keep herself from shivering at the very idea of spending even more time with Caleb.

She parked her car as close to the office building as she could manage and stood by to steady him as Caleb extracted himself from the car. Once out and balanced on his crutches, he looked up the sidewalk and sighed as if he were facing Mount Everest.

His slow pace gave her more time to study the surroundings than she'd ever had before. On her previous trips to Tanner Electronics, she'd never had reason to visit Caleb's office suite, and she looked around it with curiosity. The outer office was beautifully decorated, with deep plush carpeting and well-framed art prints on the walls. The only furniture was a big rectangular secretary's desk and the matching swivel chair.

"You can wait here." Caleb headed straight for the inner office.

"Too bad you didn't warn me to bring my knitting," Sabrina said. "Of course, since I don't knit, it wouldn't have done any good. You know, it's nice that you generally don't keep your visitors waiting. At least I assume you don't, since there's no place for them to sit. Shall I just sprawl on the floor?"

"And wrinkle your suit even more? Of course not. Use the desk."

"Won't your secretary object?"

"I don't have one."

On closer inspection, Sabrina wasn't surprised; there wasn't even a blotter on the shiny surface of the desk.

Jake appeared at the doorway of the inner office. "There you are," he said, with a note of relief in his voice. "Caleb, here's the man I was telling you about, the head of the Maxwell Agency."

Sabrina twisted around so fast she thought her neck was going to snap. *The head of the Maxwell Agency...*

The man standing in the doorway next to Jake stepped forward to offer his hand to Caleb, then—too late—noted the crutches and looked around hastily as if trying to find someone else to shake hands with. His gaze focused sharply on Sabrina, and he frowned.

He'd changed, she thought. As he neared forty, Mason Maxwell was a little heavier and even more expensively tailored, and what had been a prematurely receding hairline a few years ago had given way to a transplant job so professional that if Sabrina hadn't known he'd been balding she'd never have suspected it.

"Sabrina?" He sounded puzzled. "What are you doing here? I haven't seen you since—"

"Since the last time," she said gently.

Mason Maxwell blinked owlishly at her, and then he obviously saw, as she had, that Caleb's eyes had gone wide with surprise. "Of course," Mason said genially. "Don't worry, my dear. I wasn't going to be tactless and talk about the details right now. We'll have to get together later and catch up on all the news."

CHAPTER FIVE

CALEB said, "Anytime you're ready, Maxwell, we can start this conference and let Sabrina go about her business." He knew he sounded annoyed, but only when he saw the startled question in Jake's eyes did he realize that the cause of his aggravation could be misinterpreted. "My knee hurts like hell all of a sudden," he muttered, and swung himself on into his office without waiting for a reaction.

Behind him, Mason Maxwell gave a little laugh and said, "Of course I'm ready. I'm afraid I got carried away, thinking about old times. I'll catch you later, Sabrina."

Caleb settled into his favorite chair and stretched his leg out. He felt as if every muscle fiber in his body was vibrating. Funny, he thought, how quickly a well-rounded athlete lost his tone. Or maybe the problem was simply that swinging himself around on crutches used a whole different set of muscles than racquetball and swimming and golfing did.

Jake pushed a box over, and Caleb gratefully propped his foot on it, caught Mason Maxwell's eye and waved a hand at the chair opposite his own, while Jake perched on the edge of the desk.

Maxwell gave a careful hitch to his expensively tailored trousers and sat down. "Sorry about that," he said. "It just took me by surprise, seeing Sabrina here."

"I noticed," Caleb said dryly.

"Is she your personal assistant? Funny job for her to have. Tell you what, if she's part of the benefits package that comes with the CEO position, I just might skip the

sales pitch on my clients and put in my own application.''
He smiled broadly.

Caleb half expected him to wink. *The man certainly enjoys his own joke,* he thought. *What a charmer.*

He leaned back in his chair and said coolly, ''How many possibilities have you got for us to look at?''

Mason Maxwell sobered abruptly. ''Not as many as you might think. But don't be fooled by what may appear to be a sparse choice. It only takes one great candidate to fill a job, and we at the Maxwell Agency work very hard to create that perfect match so you don't have to.''

His little spiel was obviously well-rehearsed and so smoothly spoken that Caleb felt himself starting to zone out as if he were watching a hypnotist perform.

What old times had Mason Maxwell and Sabrina shared, Caleb wondered. And what kind of sensitive detail was it that he'd assured her he wasn't going to talk about?

There was nothing to read in the outer office except the Yellow Pages. ''He could at least have warned me to bring a magazine,'' Sabrina muttered.

Not that she'd have been doing anything more than idly leafing through it, anyway. Concentrating on the printed word would have been impossible with Mason Maxwell closeted with Caleb, telling him heaven knew what.

What ridiculous twist of fate had thrown Mason Maxwell's job-placement firm together with Tanner Electronics at precisely the moment Sabrina was caught in the middle? Last week she hadn't even been in the building; next week things would be back to normal. Any other time on the calendar, Mason could have come and gone without ever getting a hint that Sabrina Saunders existed. But no—he had to show up today.

And now that he had?

It doesn't really matter, she told herself briskly. It had been a shock to run into him, of course, and it was annoying to see him again under these conditions. But it wasn't serious. She supposed, if he was still in touch with her parents, that he might mention having seen her. But even that couldn't do more than create a fuss; they'd written her off long ago, and news about what she was doing now couldn't possibly make the family situation more difficult.

In fact, she thought, Mason had actually already done his worst by making that sly little comment in front of Caleb about not sharing the details.

Of course, Caleb would never believe that Mason had held his tongue not because he was such a perfect gentleman but because there were no intimate, embarrassing details to share....

Sabrina pulled herself up short. Why should she care what Caleb thought of her? And wasn't she making an unwarranted assumption in even believing that he'd paid any attention to what Mason had said?

Of course, there had been that sharp comment about getting down to business—but that didn't mean he'd actually listened to what Mason had said, much less been annoyed by it. Maybe Caleb had just been aggravated because the man was keeping him waiting. He'd said his knee was hurting, and it would be no wonder if he was feeling some pain after the long walk from the car and through the big building to his office at the far corner.

On second thought, however, Sabrina was more convinced by her initial appraisal of the situation. Caleb might not particularly care what Mason had said, but she was sure he'd noticed it. He was far too skilled at that sort of innuendo himself to miss it in someone else's remarks.

Of course, that didn't mean he would take it seriously. And even if he did take Mason's words at face value, it was none of Caleb's business how many men she'd known or how deeply she'd been involved with them.

In fact, she reflected, it might be an interesting pastime to see how much she could make Caleb believe. Spinning him tales about her supposed love affairs would be more fun than choosing paint samples, that was sure.

Not that she had to do either one. She certainly had no intention of actually getting wrapped up in redecorating Caleb's house. He hadn't really been serious anyway—or if he had, she concluded, he couldn't have been thinking clearly. When the time came that he was back on his feet, he'd probably be even more annoyed with her if she *had* started a renovation project—because then he'd be stuck with her till the work was finished.

Or, at least, he'd be stuck with *somebody*.

Sabrina thought about that for a long time. He had told her to go ahead with the redecoration. But what would happen if she actually followed through on that order?

As she considered all the possibilities, she found herself smiling.

The first step, of course, if she had seriously intended to renovate his house, would be to hire a professional who would put together a basic plan and bring it back for Sabrina's approval. Then Sabrina would choose from that assortment of ideas the precise colors and fabrics and designs and styles, and the real work could start.

In fact, however, under the present conditions, things would never reach that stage. She'd never have to do more than hire the professional decorator, because it would take days, maybe even weeks, for that person to gather ideas and samples. By the time that was done, Sabrina would be long gone. It would be Caleb who found himself buried in fabric swatches and paint chips.

He'd bragged that he could defend himself against anything once he was back on his feet, she remembered with a trace of malice. All she'd be doing would be giving him an opportunity to show off that skill. Right?

She pulled the Yellow Pages closer and began to study the listings of decorators and interior designers. Who sounded most able to give Caleb Tanner a challenge? Could one of these women give him the comeuppance he so desperately needed?

She was debating the relative merits of a couple of promising firms when Mason Maxwell came out of Caleb's office. Sabrina glanced toward the open door, but there was no sign of the others. She wondered if Caleb and Jake had rejected Mason's proposal altogether or if they'd asked him to step out while they discussed his candidates.

Mason leaned over the desk and planted both palms on the shiny surface. "It's a surprise to see you sitting in an office, Sabrina. I thought you were going into domestic service."

Sabrina barely looked up. "You don't need to make it sound as if I signed on to be Queen Victoria's upstairs maid."

"Didn't that work out? Or did you only threaten it in the first place because the very idea was guaranteed to make your parents go ballistic?"

"Rent-A-Wife is working out fine." *Apart from a few cash-flow problems here and there,* she thought, *and a client who doesn't mind descending to blackmail to get what he wants.*

"Then what are you doing here?" Mason sounded skeptical.

Sabrina flipped to the next Yellow Pages entry. "This particular assignment is part of the job."

Mason's eyes grew cold. "I see. Office temp work is what you prefer to what I offered you."

"Any day of the week," Sabrina said equably.

"It doesn't appear to be too tough a job. A telephone that doesn't seem to ring, no piles of memos to give you paper cuts, not even a computer keyboard to mess up your pretty manicure."

"It's pretty much what you thought I was capable of doing, isn't it, Mason? In other words, nothing much."

"Of course, I'm sure a guy like Caleb Tanner expects you to do *something* to earn your salary." His drawl was an insult in itself. "At least I offered to marry you, Sabrina."

Sabrina looked him square in the eye and asked sweetly, "Has my father ever happened to notice how crude you can be, Mason? How small-minded? How—"

She stopped as a redhead with an hourglass figure came into the room and stopped dead, obviously shocked at the sight of Sabrina. In a breathy soprano she said, "Nobody told me Caleb had a secretary now."

"That," Mason said, "is a matter of some speculation."

Sabrina ignored him. "If you're here to visit Caleb," she said, "I'm afraid he's not seeing callers this morning."

The redhead clutched the package she held—a large, flat, brightly wrapped box—and scowled childishly. "But I just wanted to bring him a get-well gift."

"I'll see that he gets it," Sabrina said.

The young woman shook her head firmly.

"Then I'll give him a message," Sabrina said patiently. "If you'd like to leave your name—"

The redhead looked past her. "Caleb!" she squealed and ran lightly across the deep carpet to the doorway of the inner office, where he'd stopped in mid-swing. She stood on tiptoe and kissed him full on the mouth. "My goodness, you look so..."

"Pale?" Caleb said carelessly. "Weak? Tragically wounded?"

The redhead giggled and confided, "Of course not. I was going to say that you look terribly sexy with those crutches."

Sabrina rolled her eyes and stood up, pushing the Yellow Pages away.

"I brought you a game, Caleb," the redhead said eagerly. "I know you'll like it. I can't wait to show you—"

"That's nice of you, Candi. Give it to Sabrina, won't you? As you can see, I can't carry anything myself."

The redhead pouted. "But wouldn't you like me to stay and show you how to play?"

Sabrina strolled over to her and held out a hand for the box. "Sorry," she said. "Recess is over, and it's naptime for our hero."

The redhead didn't relinquish the package, and she didn't look at Sabrina. "In that case, I'll bring it to your house when you're free," she told Caleb. "Tonight, maybe?"

He shrugged. "You'll have to ask Sabrina about that, Candi. Since she's the hostess in residence now, I couldn't possibly invite anyone without checking to see whether she's in the mood to entertain."

Mason nodded knowingly.

The redhead's eyes opened wide in shock. "*Her?*" she said with something close to loathing. "She's living with you?"

Caleb shifted the tip of a crutch and managed to get one arm partially around Sabrina. She couldn't quite figure out how he'd done it, but the fact remained that suddenly she was standing very close to him. "Yes, Candi," he said. "She is." He smiled at Sabrina, and his lips brushed her temple in what she thought must look like a fond caress.

Sabrina's first instinct was to duck away from that almost

scorching touch, but just in time she realized how avoidance would look to the assembled audience. And there was Mason, standing there with an I-knew-it smirk on his face....

She turned a little toward Caleb, raised a slender hand to his face and with her fingertip wiped away the smudges of the redhead's lipstick. "We can't have this, you know," she chided.

"You could always kiss it away," Caleb murmured huskily.

The mere suggestion was enough to make Sabrina sizzle with irritation, and the sparkle of humor in his eyes said he didn't think she'd do it. She stared at him, unable to turn away from that unspoken challenge.

As long as you're at it, a little demon in the back of her brain whispered, *why not go the whole nine yards and really teach him a lesson?*

Sabrina looked at him through her lashes and murmured, "And here I was thinking you wanted to keep this sort of thing private. Too bad I got all the lipstick off already—but we can always pretend." She stood on her toes and leaned closer, but instead of kissing him, she used the tip of her tongue to very slowly trace the outline of his mouth.

Before she was halfway done Sabrina knew she was in big trouble. Caleb hadn't even moved, but every muscle in his body had tensed like an overwound spring. His eyes had gone dark, and the humor that had danced there was gone.

But she wasn't fool enough to think that his reaction was because he found her caress distasteful. While his challenge had acted on her like a flame set to dry tinder, her answer to it was apparently causing him to react like a long-dormant volcano—still quiet and peaceful-looking on the outside, but with fiery lava boiling beneath the surface.

And it was causing the same kind of turmoil inside Sabrina. The contact of her tongue against his skin was producing an electrical charge that hummed painfully along every nerve in her body, her heartbeat was skipping erratically, and her ribs felt as if they'd locked tight to prevent her from ever drawing another full breath.

The trouble was, much as she'd like to back out of the situation, she couldn't stop halfway. Chickening out would only cause him to ask why she hadn't been able to finish what she'd started. And she didn't want to admit that what had started as a childish get-even prank had rocked her to her toes.

No, she'd dealt herself the hand, and now the only choice she had was to play it through—self-torture though it was.

By the time she finally stepped back, Sabrina was seeing everything in a haze of blue—something to do with an oxygen shortage, she thought vaguely.

Mason's eyebrows had gone so high they almost disappeared into his expensively restored hairline. Jake, standing just beyond the door to the inner office, was shaking his head as though it hurt.

Under her perfect makeup the redhead's skin faded to dead white and then mottled with angry color. "Congratulations," she snapped as she turned on her heel and stamped out of the office.

"If she hadn't taken that hint," Caleb said under his breath, "I was going to send out for a sledgehammer." His voice sounded as if someone had run a carpenter's rasp across it. "Let's go home, Sabrina."

Her smile felt more like a grimace. "Of course. You must be tired out, poor darling, because you're beginning to get cranky."

"No," Caleb said frankly. "I just can't wait to find out what you might be planning to do next."

In the main hallway and safely away from the executive offices, Sabrina glanced around to be sure no one was in hearing distance before she said, "Don't overdo it, Caleb."

"Saying I want to be alone with you? It's true, you know."

"Especially if the alternative is Candi and her board game," Sabrina said dryly. "I can't begin to tell you how flattered I am, to be preferred to a woman called Candi— why am I not surprised at the name?—and a board game that's no doubt X-rated. You've given me an honor that I'll treasure forever."

"If I were you," Caleb murmured, "I wouldn't talk too loudly about other people's X-rated games. If that exhibition was a sample of the kind *you* like to play—"

"Don't get any ideas. That was purely a demonstration for effect, not to be taken as an invitation."

He sighed. "That's what I was afraid you were going to say."

"Anyway, if you'll make an attempt to drag your mind off games and back to the subject, Caleb—"

"I'm all ears."

"While I'm flattered to be known as your hostess in residence—mostly because it's so much more attractive a label than bimbo of the week—I really think you'd better reconsider. If you're not careful, people will be expecting this to get serious."

"That was the general idea," Caleb reminded her.

"But you can't have thought it all the way through. You've maintained your life-style all these years by—"

"You don't need to make it sound like *that* many years," he said plaintively.

"—by making it very clear that you're not in the least interested in settling down. However, if you slip up now and let all the women in your life reach the conclusion that you're serious about me—"

"They'll leave me alone."

"No, they won't. They'll soon deduce that if you could get serious about one woman you could do it again."

Caleb pursed his lips in a soundless whistle. "You may be on to something there," he said slowly.

"Of course I am. The bottom line is, if you once let them believe that under the right circumstances—if they can play their cards perfectly—you might actually fall into the trap, you'll never again know a moment's peace. These women may not be Rhodes scholars, but in certain areas they're very sharp—and just as soon as I'm out of the way, they'll start in on you in earnest."

He paused in the center of the atrium lobby, leaned on his crutches and started to smile.

Sabrina stumbled to a halt, uneasily aware that she'd gone wrong somewhere but without a clue where he could have found a flaw in her logic. "You're taking this awfully well," she said suspiciously. "And don't tell me you planned it this way, because I won't believe you."

"Not exactly. You've pointed out a couple of trouble spots that I hadn't anticipated. But why heat myself up over something I can't change?"

"Of course you can change it. You can still tone things down, stop acting as if I'm—"

Caleb shook his head. "Not any more. Or didn't you catch what made Candi so angry? You disappoint me, Sabrina."

In her mind, Sabrina replayed the last few minutes. "She was furious because I was kissing you, but—"

Delight sparkled in his eyes once more. "Is that what you call a kiss? In that case, I can't wait to see your definition of seduction."

Sabrina tried to ignore him, despite the tinge of pink she could feel creeping into her cheeks, and kept on trying to reconstruct the scene in his office. In fact, she thought with a hint of surprise, maybe it hadn't been the kiss that had irritated Candi so, for the redhead had been incensed well before that stunt. She'd hit a peak just about the time Caleb had described Sabrina as his hostess in residence.... But why should that have upset her?

Sabrina shook her head. "I don't see it. Unless... No, you surely can't mean she was surprised I've moved in."

"Of course she was," Caleb said cheerfully. "I've always avoided that complication before. Once someone's moved in, you see, it's so messy to invite them to move *out* that I've just made it a rule never to get into that fix. But this time—"

Sabrina said, through clenched teeth, "You mean I'm the first bimbo of the week who's actually moved in with you?"

"I could quarrel with your choice of words. But in essence...yes, you are. So of course she's taking you more seriously than any of the others."

Sabrina felt herself growing livid.

"Anyway, the answer to the problem you've posed is obvious." Caleb started moving slowly once more toward the entrance. "And very simple, too. I'll just have to make sure you don't go anywhere till they've all given up and I can get a fresh start."

Mechanically, she opened the building's front door for him.

"But don't think I'm pining," Caleb added cheerfully. "With your talent for surprises, Sabrina, I suspect I'm not going to be missing out on much while I wait."

Sabrina was quiet on the drive to the house, which surprised Caleb a bit. He'd half anticipated an argument, maybe even an attempt to bargain her way clear. But the last thing he'd have expected from the very verbal Sabrina was dead silence.

He wondered why she should be so annoyed at the idea of carrying on their masquerade a little longer. Because of Mason Maxwell? Surely not; if the possibility of renewing the old times she'd shared with Maxwell had been important to Sabrina, she wouldn't have wrapped herself around Caleb for what she had so inadequately termed a kiss.

Kiss, hell, he thought inelegantly. He could feel himself getting light-headed at the memory. There was no question the woman could make blood boil—and he wasn't talking about anger.

Or maybe, he considered, that incredible display had been aimed squarely at Maxwell, instead. If he'd been the one to break off their relationship, and Sabrina had seized a chance to show him what he was missing...

Not a particularly pleasant idea, that Caleb himself might have been almost an incidental consideration in that earth-shaking embrace. On the other hand, the notion that Sabrina might actually care what that stuffed shirt Maxwell thought was almost too hilarious to contemplate.

Almost.

"Tell me about Mason Maxwell," he said.

"Why?"

"Because if I'm going to be working with him, I think I should know as much as I can about the man."

He thought she looked a trifle surprised that he hadn't put a personal spin on the question. But of course that was why he'd given the unexpected answer—in an attempt to take her off guard, to get an honest reaction rather than a calculated one.

"Are you going to be working with him?" Sabrina asked.

"I don't know. He's got a couple of decent-looking candidates, but they're not the only ones we're looking at."

"He's very good at what he does."

So much for that try, Caleb thought. "Professionally speaking," he prompted, "I'm sure that's true. What about personally?"

She looked at him with exasperation. "Why ask me? I'm not quizzing you about all the women you've dated. Of course, to be perfectly fair, I don't expect to live long enough to hear the details about all the women you've dated, so I might as well not even start down the list, but still—"

"So you did date Maxwell." He watched her catch her lower lip between her teeth and thought, *Got nailed, didn't you, Sabrina? You couldn't resist getting in a dig, and you tripped yourself up.*

"Not for very long," she said, almost too casually. "My father liked him, you see."

Caleb rubbed the nape of his neck. "And that was enough to make you dump him?"

"You obviously don't know my father. I thought if he wanted Mason in the family so badly he should adopt him instead of expecting me to be a sacrificial goat."

Caleb grinned. "I bet that attitude thrilled your dad. How'd you meet Maxwell?"

She sounded reluctant, but she answered. "I was working in a brokerage firm."

"And he was investing? Or trying to convince the boss to move on to bigger and better things?" He frowned as he recalled something Mason Maxwell had said earlier. At the time, of course, Maxwell must have been thinking that Sabrina was Caleb's secretary—but if she'd worked in an office before, why would a secretarial post be such an odd job for her to hold? How had the man said it, anyway? *Funny job for her to have,* that was it.

Caleb didn't realize he'd spoken aloud till he saw Sabrina's face tense. "And exactly why is it so strange?" Her voice was steely. "Because you think I'm constitutionally suited only to run errands and do dishes?"

Hastily, Caleb shook his head. "Nothing of the sort. It wasn't my idea in the first place—Maxwell said it, and I was just wondering why he thought being a secretary was such an odd thing for you to do."

"Oh." She didn't relax completely, he noted, but she wasn't as taut as a bowstring anymore. "Maybe it's because I wasn't sitting at the reception desk at the brokerage firm. I was running the place."

He felt his jaw drop. "Then why—"

"Why am I running errands and washing dishes these days? In a way," she said thoughtfully, "it was Mason who gave me the idea. He thought the brokerage business was stressing me out and I should stay home and do nothing more involved than pouring out his cornflakes and making sure his suits came back from the cleaners."

"He wanted you to be a trophy wife?"

Sabrina nodded. "I couldn't imagine facing Mason over the breakfast table every morning, but he was right about the stress. I realized I wanted to do something where I was in control of my own hours and could make my own decisions, while having less job pressure and more free time. And until you came along, that's about the way Rent-A-Wife was working out."

The dry note in her voice made him grin.

"It had the added advantage," she said dispassionately, "of almost giving my father a stroke when I told him I'd rather be a maid of all work than marry Mason. That's when he and my mother disowned me.''

His forehead wrinkled. "Your mother, too?"

"She hasn't had a thought independent of my father in—oh, I'd say twenty years." Sabrina parked the convertible in the drive, as close as possible to the front door of his house. "Just how far do you plan to take this demonstration, Caleb?"

He maneuvered himself out of the car, still thinking about her parents. "What demonstration?"

"Do you anticipate actually announcing an engagement?"

Misgiving flickered across his mind. The question sounded awfully calm—perhaps a shade too calm. And with it coming straight on top of the blithe revelation that she was not precisely what she'd seemed, he couldn't help but be wary. Was she plotting? Trying to maneuver him into a corner where he'd be committed to the one thing he'd avoided at all costs for so long?

No, he told himself. She'd tried to sidestep being involved at all, hadn't she?

And yet, that embrace in his office had made quite a statement. Even though she'd promptly followed it with a warning, the fact was she hadn't said anything till after he'd announced himself in public. And the net effect—

You are seeing spooks where they do not exist, Caleb told himself. "I don't think we need to go that far."

"So we're supposedly living together with no intention of making it legal," she mused.

Why the cool, clear definition should set his teeth on edge was more than Caleb could understand. "It's a whole lot more definite than I've been with any other woman, so I think—"

"If you're telling me not to press my luck, don't let it

make you sweat,'' Sabrina remarked. "It's going to be bad enough having everyone I know think I've lost my mind enough to live with you. Having to explain that I was actually such a fool that I believed a diamond ring on my finger would tie you down—'' She shuddered delicately.

Caleb grinned. "You're a woman in a thousand, Sabrina.''

"And you," she said under her breath, "are certainly the man who's got enough experience to know.''

CHAPTER SIX

As Sabrina came into the living room on Saturday morning, she was mentally rehearsing all the arguments why Caleb would be better off if he stayed at home to rest rather than coming with her for Cassie's bridal shower.

Even as she marshaled her facts, however, she was hoping that he'd have dozed off so she could escape quietly instead—because forty-eight hours in Caleb Tanner's company had left Sabrina with the uncomfortable feeling that she was more likely to win a Nobel prize in chemistry than to change his mind, no matter how convincing her arguments.

She tiptoed into the room, but Caleb heard her and looked up with a grin. "Just the person I've been waiting for," he said. "Since I can't reach my foot, I need Princess Charming to help me get into my glass slipper."

Sabrina eyed the white running shoe he held up. Not exactly dainty footgear, she thought. Could she really put both her feet into one of Caleb's shoes, or did it only look that way?

"As a slapstick comedy, it's got possibilities," she admitted. She pulled up a stool, and he stretched out his immobilized leg so she could slide the shoe into place. "Next Halloween you could go to the party in a ball gown—white satin, I think, to coordinate with the shoe—"

"You have to be kidding."

Sabrina looked at him thoughtfully for a long moment. "Oh, I see. I didn't know, of course, that you had a phobia about white satin altogether. I thought it was just the idea of a *woman* wearing white satin that made you run the other direction."

Caleb shook his head. "If I go to the party—if, in fact, there's a Halloween party at all—I won't be wearing satin. I'll just dress up in a full-body cast at the outset so I'll be prepared."

"For me, you mean." Sabrina kept her voice level. "Who says I'm going to be there at all? And what are you saying, *if* there's a party? By then, with your revolving-door life-style, you could even be back on good terms with Angelique." She pulled his shoelaces as tight as she could.

"Could be," he said cheerfully. "If you wouldn't mind loosening that knot a little, Sabrina—just enough to restore the blood flow to my toes..."

"Heaven forbid it should come untied," Sabrina said. "If you were to trip over a dangling shoelace and crack up your other knee—"

"How sweet of you to be so concerned about me."

She went straight on. "I'd never hear the end of it. I'd probably find myself waiting on you well into the next decade."

He looked intrigued by the possibility, but he didn't pursue it. "Even loose, these will be better than the loafers I was wearing yesterday. I'm hoping I can keep my balance a little more easily and maybe even put a bit of weight on my leg."

There went excuse number one, Sabrina thought—that some of the floors in her condo were covered with ceramic tile and thus were too slick to be safe for a man on crutches. However, she mused, she wouldn't get anywhere at all with her campaign to leave him behind if she didn't even try, would she?

"I think," she suggested, "considering the way your knee swelled yesterday after you'd been up for a while, that you'd be better off to stay home, keep it elevated and let Jennings bring you ice packs.''

''Jennings doesn't have the same touch with an ice pack that you do.'' Caleb shifted to the edge of the couch and reached for his crutches.

Sabrina admitted, ''He's probably not as tempted as I am to ram one down your throat.''

''Exactly. Sabrina, you surely can't expect me to lie here and stare at these four walls all day.''

''I'll grant that they're not the most attractive walls ever built, but if you really can't stand them, why did you buy the house in the first place?''

''Because I fell in love with the attic,'' Caleb said promptly. ''I hardly even looked at the rest of the house, and I certainly didn't anticipate being couch-bound for weeks on end staring at the plaster down here.''

''It's not going to be weeks. It's barely been two days now, and you're already much better.''

''All right, it only *feels* like weeks. But I'm hardly what you could call fully healed.''

''Wait a minute. You said yourself you were ready to try putting weight on it.'' She paused and added solicitously, ''Though, now that I think about it, you are still looking awfully pale.''

''I'm glad to know you're paying attention.''

''And as long as you're in such bad shape,'' Sabrina pointed out, ''you really shouldn't be gallivanting around to bridal showers.''

There was a brief silence. She peeked at him and was a little surprised by the gleam she saw in his eyes.

''That's not a bad idea, at all,'' Caleb murmured. ''As a matter of fact, it solves all the problems.''

''What does?'' Sabrina's tone was wary.

"You offering to pass up the bridal shower and lie here with me."

"I said nothing of the kind!"

"With that kind of entertainment I'm sure it will feel like no time at all till I'm well. And I'll probably forget all about the walls, too."

The low, sultry tone of his voice not only implied that she could make him ignore a whole lot more than walls, but it set off a sort of sensual storm in Sabrina's brain. Suddenly she could not only see and hear him, but even though there was a foot of empty space between them, she could taste him and feel his touch against her skin.

And from the slight but appreciative widening of his eyes, she could tell Caleb knew the effect he was having every bit as well as she did.

There was no sense in scolding herself about it, Sabrina thought. Of course she'd reacted to him; she was a perfectly normal human being, and Caleb Tanner was a couple of hundred pounds of smooth and practiced sex appeal. Any woman who was at least semiconscious would have done the same.

For that matter, Sabrina told herself, a begonia plant would probably get all hot and bothered if Caleb looked at it the way he'd just looked at her.

What set her apart from the other women who must have suffered exactly the same symptoms from a close encounter with Caleb, however, was that Sabrina knew she was no different from any of them—at least in his mind. She understood perfectly well that causing excited discomfort in every female who crossed his path came as natural to Caleb as breathing did.

It didn't mean he'd gone to extra effort where she was concerned. It didn't mean she was special. It was absolutely nothing for her to get hysterical about.

The best thing she could do, she thought, was to put the brakes on immediately, just to make sure the impression he was getting at the moment didn't settle into his mind as accepted fact. Just to make sure he realized that her reaction to him hadn't overwhelmed her common sense.

Very slowly, as if she was fighting an irresistible force and gradually—despite her best efforts—losing ground, Sabrina leaned forward until her lips almost met Caleb's and she could feel his breath, his warmth, against her face. "If you're suggesting I sleep with you—" she whispered.

"I wasn't exactly inviting you for a nap, but—"

She said, each word soft but distinct, "Not on your life."

She was close enough to feel his lips purse, and it took all her self-control to keep from jerking away from him. What an idiotic, short-sighted idea that had been, to challenge him like that. If he ignored what she'd said and kissed her instead...

But he didn't. "Pity," he murmured. "What a waste of an afternoon, when we could have such fun together."

She sat back a few inches and tried to keep her voice matter-of-fact. "I thought you said the moon would have to turn to liverwurst before you wanted to sleep with me, anyway."

Caleb shrugged. "I guess, now that I can't sky dive or race my motorcycle, I must be missing the element of danger in my life, so I'm looking for something just as risky to do."

"That's a relief. I was afraid you'd decided you weren't immune to me after all."

"Oh, no." Caleb's tone was reassuring. "I never said you weren't attractive, you know, just that I was in no danger of losing my mind where you're concerned."

"I'll try not to forget that," Sabrina said dryly. "Particularly in those moments when it seems you're losing your mind altogether.''

She'd forgotten how long it took for Caleb to insert himself into her convertible, and by the time they reached her condominium complex she was nearly half an hour late and Paige was leaning against the front fender of her minivan in the parking lot, arms folded across her chest.

Sabrina swore under her breath.

Paige came up to the convertible as Caleb was levering himself out. ''I was starting to get worried about you, Sabrina,'' she said mildly. Her gaze focused on Caleb, and her voice dropped as she fell into step beside Sabrina. ''And now that I see what kept you, I'm even more concerned.''

Sabrina sighed. She opened the front door and stopped, startled by the mess on the brightly tiled floor that set off one corner of the living room as an entrance hall.

When she'd run in yesterday—with Caleb waiting in the car—to grab a few clothes, she'd simply stepped over the few pieces of mail that had been dropped through the slot in the door. Now it looked as if an entire truck had backed straight up to the condo and unloaded. She gathered an armful of paper so Caleb could safely edge by without catching his crutches, and she dumped the stack on the coffee table.

Paige raised her eyebrows. ''And how long has it been since you've been home, Sabrina?''

''My fault,'' Caleb said. ''I just can't bear to be without her, you know. And in my helpless condition—''

Sabrina pointed. ''You. On the couch. Right now.''

Caleb gave a soundless whistle. ''Domination, too? Is there any kinky sideline you're not expert in, Sabrina?''

Sabrina ignored him. ''Let's start in the kitchen, Paige.''

She led the way. "Did you make a list of what needs to be done? Heaven knows I don't know where to begin."

"Yes, I made a list—and I put you at the top of it. Sabrina, what are you thinking of?"

Rent-A-Wife, Sabrina thought. Paige would certainly understand the reasoning that had gotten Sabrina into this mess. All three of the partners had worked hard to build this business—too hard for any of them to take lightly the threatened loss of a major client.

On the other hand, the three of them were friends, almost family, as well as partners. Sabrina knew if she told Paige the truth—that Caleb had blackmailed her into being his shield from the bimbo contingent—her partner would be furious, and every last one of Paige's protective instincts would kick into high gear. Rent-A-Wife would be forgotten, overshadowed by the personal cost to Sabrina. As a result, Paige would probably rip into Caleb like a den full of tigers—and they'd soon be short a client despite Sabrina's best efforts.

But if Sabrina didn't tell the truth—if instead she simply let things ride by pretending to be just another of Caleb's bimbos... No, that option wasn't any better. Paige was still likely to blow her stack and tell him off.

So what was left?

Play the part, Sabrina told herself. If she could make Paige believe she was truly and absolutely serious about the man, she might scrape by. Whatever Paige might say to Sabrina in the guise of getting her to take a second look before she actually leaped off the cliff, she'd at least be polite to Caleb—rather than take the risk that attacking him would prompt Sabrina to defend him.

This was all getting far too complicated, Sabrina thought. Her head ached just thinking about it.

"What's come over you?" Paige demanded. "Of all the

men who have been nuts about you, Sabrina, why choose this one?''

"Maybe because he's nuts about me?" She hadn't intended to phrase it as a question, but it came out that way.

"If you think that, you are seriously delusional. Do you know what the staff at Tanner calls his house behind his back? Bedside Manor. Sabrina, if you honestly believe you're going to be the only woman in Caleb Tanner's life—''

A cold shudder ran through Sabrina's bones at the very idea. Hastily, in an effort to disguise the reaction, she reached for the teakettle. "I'm going to make myself something hot to drink," she said. "How about you? It feels like the furnace isn't working quite right in here."

Paige put a hand on Sabrina's arm. "Honey, I don't want to see you get your heart broken!''

"Believe me," Sabrina said steadily, "it isn't going to be.''

Paige sighed. "Which only means you don't want to talk about it, I suppose.''

"Coffee or hot chocolate?" Sabrina asked. "And I wonder if I shouldn't go light the gas log for Caleb.''

"I should say he's hot-blooded enough to keep the better part of Alaska from freezing all by himself," Paige muttered.

Sabrina smothered a smile as she turned away. But when she thought about it, she decided the comment hadn't really been all that funny. Why was Paige so down on Caleb? Maybe it was just a dislike of his life-style. Rent-A-Wife had a few clients who could be classified as playboys, and Paige didn't hold much brief for any of them. In fact, Sabrina thought, Paige suffered from a mistrust of men in general. But neither of those things really explained why she reacted so strongly to Caleb.

What was there about Caleb that had set Paige's teeth on edge? The subconscious recognition that he was threatening Sabrina? Or something else—something much more than that?

Was Paige drawn to him herself? If so, she might be trying to fight off the attraction by finding fault with everything about him.

In the two years Sabrina had known her, Paige hadn't shown a flicker of partiality for any man who crossed her path. Sabrina told herself firmly that it was hardly likely Caleb would be the exception. If Paige fell for anyone...

Sabrina's mind boggled at the idea. She couldn't begin to imagine what kind of man Paige might fall for, but she hoped, for Paige's sake, that it wouldn't be somebody like Caleb Tanner. Still, attraction—as well as the attempt to deny its reality—could conceal itself in all sorts of disguises.

And there was no accounting for the chemistry between two people, either. Just look at Jake and Cassie, Sabrina reminded herself. Both were loners, with a long-established habit of not depending on anyone. Both had fully intended to stay that way. And yet a week from today they'd be married....

"You're looking very thoughtful," Caleb said.

Sabrina glanced at him, sprawled at ease on her cream-colored brocade couch, and thought for an instant she was seeing double. *Two* Calebs? Two smiling faces? Two sets of sparkling blue eyes?

The second one, she realized, was on the cover of the magazine he was reading, and at the angle he was holding it, the photograph was almost as large as life. *And only slightly more predictable,* she thought. The magazine must be one of the bunch she'd picked up by the front door when they came in; she'd certainly not seen it before.

"It was awfully nice of you to get this issue," Caleb said.

"Why? So you can preen over the publicity and admire your sexy smile?"

"Do you really think it's sexy?" He demonstrated, and for an instant looked eerily like the magazine cover.

Sabrina could have bit off her tongue. If there was one thing she should have learned by now, it was that Caleb didn't miss a nuance—as long as it could be made to sound suggestive. Why couldn't she just keep her mouth shut?

"That subscription is a leftover from my days as a broker, Caleb. If I'd known you were going to be on the cover I'd have cancelled it, believe me."

He shook his head sadly. "Temper, temper. I did flip through the article to check whether they quoted me accurately, but that isn't the reason I appreciate the magazine. It's amazing, the things you can find in the fine print. Do you have a phone that'll stretch over here?"

Sabrina handed him the cordless from her desk. "It's not one of the most secure models, I'm afraid. The frequency can be intercepted. So if this is top-secret business—"

"Not exactly. I'm just enrolling you in the gift-wrap-of-the-month club."

She frowned. "I didn't know there was such a thing."

"You must have heard about it. Every four weeks they send you a new piece of risqué lingerie."

"That's what you call gift wrap? Don't you dare."

"Why not? Of course, that satin nightshirt of yours—you must already belong." He flipped the magazine open and ran his finger down the column.

He was not studying the classified section, Sabrina noted with relief. It wasn't even an advertisement he was looking at, but one of the news profiles. So much for the gift-wrap-of-the-month club; that had simply been Caleb's way of dodging the question about whether his call was important business.

Why was she so gullible, anyway? And why should she be surprised that he hadn't rushed to confide in her?

"I'll get out of your way so you can make your call in private," she said. Her voice was a trifle tight.

He obviously noticed it. "No hurry. Sit down a minute."

"I really should get busy. Paige is already working on the food, and I left the teakettle on the stove. Besides, I need to clean and dust before the party, and—"

"It's a nice place you've got here. Your business must be doing pretty well, after all."

Warily, Sabrina surveyed him. What on earth was he getting at? Should she exaggerate Rent-A-Wife's standing, or downplay it? Admitting they had cash-flow problems from time to time would only tell him how important the Tanner contract was, and it would encourage him to step up the pressure on her. But if she bragged that they were doing fine and didn't need Tanner, he might take her at her word. Worse yet, he might conclude that she was cooperating with his blackmail scheme for reasons of her own, not because they desperately needed the business.

Now I know how a pet hamster feels, Sabrina thought, *running round and round his wheel and getting nowhere fast.*

"It's doing all right," she said carefully. "But as a matter of fact, I bought the condo while I was still at the brokerage."

"I like it. It's not fluffy."

That sounded like a man, Sabrina thought.

"So how long is it going to take you to get my house in shape? You know, paint and curtains and furniture and stuff."

Stuff, she thought helplessly. "You're actually thinking

about doing it? Considering that I haven't even called a decorator—''

"Do you need one?" He looked around. "Who did this?"

"I did," she admitted. "While I was still working as a broker, I could afford to buy the place but I didn't have time to bother with decorating. After I quit, I had lots of time but a shortage of money—so I did it myself."

"Well, this is what I want. How much can you do by— say—next week?"

"Next *week?* Are you hallucinating, or are you really that naive?"

"We'll be interviewing prospects for the CEO position next week, and I thought it would be good to talk to them over dinner—in a social setting."

"Call the Pinnacle."

"Why use a restaurant when I have a house?"

"Because you have a hospital bed in your dining room!"

He shrugged. "So buy a table. What's the matter? It was your idea originally for me to entertain at home—you wanted me to invite Mason Maxwell, remember? Having a small group to dinner will be more private and more intimate than a restaurant, and there'll be a better chance to tell what someone's really like."

"Yes," Sabrina agreed. "Showing them your house will let you get a good handle on their diplomatic skills. Except, I suppose, that you still won't know if they're exceptionally tactful, or totally unobservant, or very good liars."

"So that's decided," he said cheerfully. "How much can you have done by next—oh, let's say, Tuesday?"

Sabrina stared at him. "That's only four days," she pointed out. "*If* I count today. By then, I can—oh, I can disconnect the electrical power and buy a dozen candles.

That would improve the looks of your dining room a thousand percent.''

Caleb smiled. "I have confidence in you. And just think what a job like this will do for Rent-A-Wife's reputation."

"Yeah," Sabrina muttered. "That thought had already occurred to me."

Sabrina was perched high atop a ladder, brushing forest-green paint onto the newly scrubbed dining room wall, and Paige was just dipping a brand-new roller into the paint tray when Cassie pushed open the door from the front hallway and looked in.

"Obviously I've found the right place," she said, and dropped a bundle on the plastic-draped hospital bed, which sat in one corner of the room. "I brought all the drop cloths and brushes I could find."

"Great." Sabrina dipped her brush again. "With all three of us working, we should be able to do this in a few hours. What do you think so far?"

Cassie shot a look around the room. "Well, since you ask... Isn't it going to be a little dark in here?" She opened her bundle and began to wrap a protective scarf around her mass of curly red hair.

"Believe me, darkness will do nothing but improve this room," Sabrina said.

"The proportions aren't bad," Paige commented. "Refinish the crown molding and wainscoting, hang a nice damask wallpaper, put up some lacy curtains, and it would be quite an attractive room."

"And if you can pull it off in time for a dinner party tomorrow evening," Sabrina said, "you may have a bonus. So just wave your magic wand, Paige, and then we can all quit work and go out for lunch."

"Sorry, I had to send the wand in for repairs. What about

opening those doors so some air can circulate? You look hot already up there, Sabrina.''

Sabrina shook her head. ''Caleb's going to have a meeting just across the hall, starting any minute. Since the living room is so open, we'll have to keep the dining room closed up.''

''Or else listen to a bunch of engineers talk,'' Cassie said. ''It's the regular Monday morning staff briefing. Jake said he'd be here.''

Sabrina looked thoughtfully at her. Tradition said that all brides were beautiful, but in Sabrina's opinion, Cassie was setting a new standard. Just saying her fiancé's name was enough to make her radiant. But it wasn't the fragile flicker of excitement that lit her face, it was a steady, solid glow— something that wasn't going to vanish the moment the exhilaration of the wedding day was past. It would last, and grow, through good times and bad....

The explanation was perfectly simple, Sabrina knew. Cassie was happy. Cassie was contented. Cassie knew exactly what she wanted, and she'd found it.

Cassie, she thought irritably, was incredibly lucky.

It wasn't that she begrudged her partner's happiness, Sabrina told herself hastily, for she didn't. She was glad Cassie and Jake had found each other. Her nose was only out of joint because she was having to pretend to a similar kind of feeling just now, and because the contrast between the real item and the fraudulent performance was such a painful one. That was all.

''Where do I start?'' Cassie asked.

''We left the fireplace wall with all the nooks and crannies for you,'' Paige said. ''That's what you get for being late.''

''I'm not late, exactly,'' Cassie argued. She reached for a fresh gallon of paint and an opener. ''I was on Rent-A-

Wife business, washing Ben Orcutt's dishes—and it was a
job that couldn't be put off any longer, believe me.''

Sabrina shuddered. ''Didn't you tell me about almost
needing a gas mask for that job once?''

''Not for dishes. That was the time I cleaned out his
refrigerator. But I think he waits till every cup and spoon
in the apartment is dirty before he calls for help. Some of
them weren't even really dishes, they were throwaway trays
from freezer meals.''

''I think,'' Paige said, ''that he gets everything he owns
dirty on purpose, to make a big enough job to justify calling
us in. Maybe he's really just lonely.''

''Wow.'' Cassie stared at her. ''Mark this day on the
calendar—Paige makes a sympathetic comment about a
man. Never mind that Ben Orcutt's on the shady side of
sixty, he's still male.''

''I thought he was older than that,'' Paige said.

Cassie gave a push to the hospital bed. ''What are you
going to do about furniture, Sabrina? Move your dining
room set over?''

Paige's eyes opened wide. ''That's crazy.''

''Why?'' Cassie asked reasonably. ''The set will get here
sooner or later, anyway. Why should Sabrina go buy another one when she already owns an heirloom?''

''Doesn't Caleb own anything?'' Paige shook her head.
''Scratch that—stupid question. Maybe the previous owners
left things you could use. There's an attic, isn't there?''

''Oh, yes,'' Sabrina said airily. ''It's the pièce de résis-
tance of the house, as far as Caleb is concerned—but there
aren't any antiques up there, just his model railroad.''

Paige said, ''You mean a toy train?''

''If you can call it a toy when it threatens to take up the
whole third floor, yes.''

Cassie grinned. "At least it's a hobby that will keep him at home."

"Unlike his women," Paige muttered. Then she sighed. "I'm sorry, Sabrina. I'm just afraid for you, and it makes me grumpy. It's bad enough you've moved in, but at least you can carry everything out in a suitcase. The dining room set puts things in another league entirely. If you and Caleb have a fight, he could hold it hostage."

Sabrina's conscience pinged, and she had to remind herself of all the reasons she'd opted not to tell Paige and Cassie the truth. *This will be over very soon,* she thought. And once the supposed relationship was broken off and Sabrina made it obvious that she'd come through the experience completely unscathed, her partners would soon forget the whole thing. Much sooner than they'd forgive Caleb for blackmail....

"How many people are you having?" Cassie asked practically.

"We've ended up with eight. You and Jake, Caleb and me, the production manager and his date—"

"He's not still dating that bimbo friend of Angelique's, is he?" Cassie sounded like the voice of doom.

"I'm afraid so. And then there's the prospect, of course—"

"And his wife?"

Sabrina shook her head. "I don't know if he's married, but he's coming stag to this affair. Which means I really could use an extra woman to balance the table."

Cassie's eyes narrowed. "I don't suppose Paige would like—"

Sabrina said, "I was waiting for just the right moment to ask. I need somebody who'll be pleasant and charming but won't try to annex him, in case he's already spoken for."

"That description is Paige to the life," Cassie agreed.

"I'd rather be in the kitchen." As if to punctuate the point, Paige put her roller down and popped the lid off a paint can.

"I suppose that could be arranged, too," Sabrina said. "Jennings would love to have a helping hand or three. I don't think Caleb's given a dinner party in the whole time Jennings has worked for him."

"Be a sport, Paige," Cassie urged. "It won't become a habit, you know. Even if Caleb throws this kind of tryout for every top contender, there are only three of them. And one's a woman, so Sabrina won't need an extra that night—"

"Really?" Sabrina said. She climbed off her ladder to reach for a damp rag. "A woman?"

Cassie looked at her oddly. "Caleb didn't tell you about that?"

Sabrina caught herself too late. It was only reasonable of Cassie to assume—especially since she herself so obviously knew the details—that Sabrina would have heard them, too. She was the official hostess, after all. "He probably tried, but I was thinking about curtains or something instead."

Deep in Paige's tote bag, a cell phone rang, and Paige set the paint can down. "Rent-A-Wife," she said, and then, "Hi, Mother. What is it?" She balanced the phone between shoulder and ear so she could pick up the paint again to refill her tray.

"Eileen probably wants her to come home to change the television channel," Cassie said under her breath. "So has Caleb told you anything about the guy they're interviewing tomorrow?"

"Not much," Sabrina admitted. "Just that he's in Denver to be honored at some special event, so this was the best time to talk to him about the job. Caleb saw the honor written up in a magazine, and that gave him the idea of asking him to dinner while he was here.''

"I guess it's not just the best time to pitch Tanner to him," Cassie said, "but the only time. He's not particularly eager to leave his current situation, so he's certainly not going to come rushing back here for an interview."

"But if he's not interested—" Sabrina began.

She half-heard Paige remonstrating. "I'll get to it as soon as I can, Mother, but with everything else that's going on…"

Cassie said, "That's going to be the challenge—finding a way to *make* him be interested. Austin Weaver's supposed to be a management genius."

A dull thump behind them made both Sabrina and Cassie wheel around.

The almost-full paint can had slipped from Paige's hands and was lying in the tray. Forest-green paint gurgled from the can, brimmed the tray and overflowed the edges to become an inexorable puddle.

Sabrina saw the paint seeping between the layers of plastic drop cloths toward the carpet beneath and made a grab for the can to keep any more from flowing out. Her shoulder hit Paige's arm, knocking her cell phone loose. It spiraled downward till the flat back of the phone smacked into the paint, sending a forest-green surge outward.

Sabrina set the can upright and watched in paralyzed dismay as the paint gushed through the cracks where one drop cloth met another. The carpet began to turn forest green in patches and lines. She put both hands to her face and only realized when she felt wetness that her palms were covered with paint.

"No," Paige said. "This can't be happening."

"It's all right," Sabrina said. She hardly recognized the

pained squeak as her own voice. "The carpet was old. Practically worn out. It needed to be torn up."

"It wasn't the carpet I was thinking about," Paige said. "That's two cell phones in less than a week."

"And I killed both of them," Sabrina said drearily.

Cassie shook her head. "You get credit for the first one, no question. But this one I'm laying squarely at Eileen's door for upsetting Paige like that. You know, guys, it's just not fair. I've got Jake, and I'm happier now than I've ever been. Sabrina's got Caleb."

In a manner of speaking, Sabrina thought.

"But poor Paige," Cassie went on. "You have to deal with Eileen day in and day out. Sabrina, honey," she said with determination, "we have got to do something about Paige!"

CHAPTER SEVEN

MOST of the regular Monday morning staff meeting was taken up by routine matters, and Caleb found himself smothering a yawn as he listened to the discussion. Jake had been dead on target, suggesting Caleb hire someone to deal with the details of day-to-day management in order to be free for experimentation, which was both his first love and his strongest asset.

If only they'd managed to hire someone already, Caleb thought, he could shunt this everlasting discussion off on the new CEO, and Caleb could get down to real work. One of his favorite and most productive young engineers was sitting to one side of the living room; Caleb had noticed the moment the young man had walked in that he was practically bursting with excitement. What Eric was so enthusiastic about, Caleb didn't know, but he was as eager to ask as the young man obviously was to talk about it—if the meeting didn't drag on so long that he lost all his zeal.

Caleb glanced at his watch for the fourth time in ten minutes and had to admit that in truth the meeting hadn't gone on all that long; it was simply his impatience with administrative detail that made it seem as if he'd been locked up all morning. And that particular problem—his impatience—was getting worse. As long as there hadn't seemed to be an alternative, he'd gritted his teeth and dealt with the routine. But now that he knew an escape was almost within sight...

If one of the top three prospects was the perfect fit he hoped for, Caleb could be free of the drag of office routine

117

by the end of the month. He wondered which of the three would be successful. The retired army colonel who was Jake's choice from the stack of applications they'd received? The young woman whose résumé Mason Maxwell had put forward? Or his preference, the man he'd run across in Sabrina's magazine over the weekend—the man who was coming to dinner on Tuesday?

Caleb had to admit that his choice was the longest shot of all. Austin Weaver's name was known across corporate America, and it was always spoken in a respectful hush—except perhaps by the people who'd come up against him in business deals and walked away the loser.

Considering the position and power Weaver wielded, Caleb knew it wasn't going to be easy to interest him in an electronics firm that—though it showed great promise—was still on the small side. It wasn't going to be easy to interest him in moving halfway across the country to relocate in Denver.

To tell the truth, it hadn't been easy to interest Austin Weaver in coming to dinner. Caleb had had to exercise considerable charm to get through the layers of secretaries, and then more charm to convince the man to extend his stay in Denver for a few hours after receiving his award so he could at least take a look at Tanner Electronics.

Jake thought he was wasting his time, and Caleb had to admit that Austin Weaver could probably write his own ticket with nearly any major industry in the country. Still, what did any of them have to lose but a few hours?

Besides, Caleb thought, the coincidence of Weaver being in Denver at this very moment was just too good to pass up. Austin Weaver had been in his current job for close to five years, and there was always the chance that he was starting to get itchy, ready for a change and a new challenge.

And as Caleb had pointed out to Jake, for a man who'd spent his career with enormous and well-established companies, growing a small electronics firm would definitely be a challenge.

Always assuming, of course, that they hit it off. No matter how powerful the man's name, Caleb wasn't foolish enough to hire him on the strength of it. Unless that elusive thing called chemistry was right, Caleb would be better off to promote the janitor than to hire Austin Weaver.

There had been thumps and bangs from across the hall throughout his meeting, but Caleb had successfully tuned them out—until he heard a muffled shriek. His gaze met Jake's across the circle, and it was apparent they were thinking exactly the same thing. *What's Sabrina done now?*

Caleb excused himself, reached for his crutches and swung lightly across the hallway. He pushed the dining room door open with his shoulder, but prudently he didn't rush inside.

Whatever had happened, at first glance it didn't appear to have damaged any of the three young women in the room, and the connoisseur in him automatically noted what a delightful picture they formed in their work clothes.

The back view of Sabrina in close-fitting jeans was particularly worthwhile, Caleb thought. She was bending over something on the floor—no doubt the source of the trouble and the reason for the shriek. He'd have to check that out in a minute, he decided. Find out exactly what was going on. But only after he'd looked his fill at slender hips and legs a mile long....

She straightened and turned, mopping her face with a cloth of some sort. Caleb blinked and looked again. No, his eyes weren't deceiving him—her cheeks had turned green.

He glanced at the others. The front of Paige's sweatshirt

looked as if she'd been bodysurfing through a forest-green lake. Only Cassie seemed unscathed.

Caleb shook his head. "Is this all the damage you can do?" he asked gently. "I'm disappointed, Sabrina. I thought surely with three gallons of paint you could cover the whole—"

She stopped mopping her face and threw the towel at him.

Caleb had never realized that a wadded-up wet piece of terry cloth could move with the same speed, force and grace as a World Series fastball. He knew if he didn't get out of the way, he was likely to be sorry.

Automatically, forgetting that he wasn't quite up to rac-quetball-style maneuvers at the moment, Caleb tried to duck to one side. The rubber tip of his crutch came down on the edge of a plastic drop cloth and skidded out of control. Without the crutch to provide support, his foot unexpectedly took his entire weight. The shock telegraphed through his injured knee, and Caleb swore and crumpled to the floor. As he went down, the back of his head clipped the doorjamb. The wet towel smacked against the woodwork directly above him and slid down to drape itself over his hair.

Caleb had never before been hit so hard he'd seen stars— in fact, he'd thought they were a metaphorical invention. But he was seeing them now. *Shooting* stars.

Sabrina dropped to her knees beside him. She looked absolutely white except for the stains on her cheeks. Her eyes, as green as the paint, were wide with horror, and she was bending over him with her hand at his throat. *Is she trying to finish the job by choking me?* he wondered a little hazily.

Then he noticed the way the neckline of her plaid flannel shirt drooped, and he forgot everything else. Under the practical work clothes, Sabrina was wearing a wisp of a black lace bra, and as she leaned over him, Caleb had the best seat in town for a truly delightful show.

Her fingertips were resting against the base of his throat. ''Your pulse is racing,'' she said breathlessly.

He didn't stop looking. ''Fancy that.'' His voice sounded gruff, and his throat felt dry.

Sabrina drew in a sharp breath and sat on her heels, one hand clutching the neckline of her shirt. ''If you weren't already wounded, I'd slap you,'' she muttered.

''For looking? I thought you were being an angel of mercy, trying to take my mind off my pain. And honey, what a way to take it off—''

She pulled the wet towel over his eyes and leaped to her feet.

Caleb sighed. It had been nice while it lasted.

He didn't think he was suffering from a concussion; at least, the shooting stars had gone away. It was odd, though, he thought, that as experienced as he was with feminine attire, he'd gone all fuzzy-brained like that over a mere glimpse of a black-lace push-up bra.

Perhaps it had been the contrast between the practical flannel shirt and the peekaboo lingerie. That made sense, he decided; he'd have predicted a sports bra, and that sight wouldn't have intrigued him nearly as much as had the completely unexpected scrap of black lace.

And it was certainly true that a glimpse was often more titillating than a full view, especially in a crowded room where he was the only one in a position to spy.

But it was still odd, he thought, that he'd reacted quite so strongly.

By late evening, the smell of paint still hung heavily in the dining room, even though all four walls were dry to the touch. Sabrina was perched atop her ladder by the windows at the front of the house, trying to even out the folds of a white lace panel she'd draped over a makeshift curtain rod, when Caleb limped in.

She stopped tugging at the lace and watched in remorse as he sank down on the side of the hospital bed, still draped in plastic but once more sitting squarely in the center of the room. Perhaps it was the glare of the chandelier, but he still looked pale, hours after his fall.

"I'm really sorry," Sabrina said.

Caleb shrugged. "It's as much my fault as yours. I violated my own rule—to keep my distance when you're armed and dangerous—so I probably deserve what I got."

She bit her tongue to keep from agreeing with him. *Is this all the damage you can do?* He should be grateful she hadn't wrapped a crutch around his head for that remark instead of just a paint-stained towel.

He'd certainly been careful to follow his self-imposed regulations for the rest of the day, though. Ever since a couple of the guys attending the meeting had helped Caleb from the floor and into the living room to the safety of his couch, Sabrina had hardly seen him, and he hadn't called for her once. She could have been miles away, and he wouldn't have known it.

She could have walked out, and he wouldn't even have missed her. So much for the idea that he needed her dancing attendance on him hand and foot. If it hadn't been for the damned dinner party tomorrow, she'd be tempted to do it.

Of course, a deal was still a deal—and if Sabrina didn't hold up her end of the bargain, Rent-A-Wife would suffer the consequences.

In fact, she thought moodily, she'd probably made the whole situation worse with that stunt today. Losing his balance, falling down and cracking his head on the door-jamb... Though she hadn't caused Caleb's injuries, exactly, throwing the towel *had* been the instigating factor.

She supposed, when it came right down to it, that she should be grateful he hadn't assumed she'd done it on purpose, in some kind of convoluted effort to free herself by prompting him to order her out of the house. If he'd believed she'd planned it, Caleb would probably have not only sent her packing but held to his word to ruin Rent-A-Wife.

But of course, he was stuck right now, too, with an important dinner party scheduled and his house a wreck.

"You could still cancel this dinner, you know," she said.

"After all the trouble it took to line it up, why would I want to?"

"Well, I didn't mean cancel, exactly. But you could still move it somewhere else."

"A place that doesn't have psychedelic carpet, for instance."

Sabrina looked at the damp splotches of forest-green paint that marred the worn beige carpet. From atop her ladder, one of them looked like a witch on a broomstick, another like a leopard in mid-leap coming straight at her. *Which says something about my state of mind,* she thought. *This is no time to take an inkblot test—I'd end up in the psych ward for sure.*

She said slowly, "I'm afraid the best I can do about the carpet is have it pulled up tomorrow and rent a really big throw rug to cover up the marred floor."

"I'm sure that will look nice alongside the rented furniture." His tone was level.

"Look, I know you think it's a waste of money to rent stuff, Caleb, but it really does make sense. Shopping for what you like takes time, which you haven't got. And the odds are when you find what you want, it won't be in stock and will have to be ordered, so—''

"I like your furniture."

"My dining room set is an antique. You can't find that sort of thing every day. Besides, you don't want to be locked into my choices." *And Paige is right, I'd be a fool to take a chance that you'd hold my furniture hostage—even if she's wrong about the reasons you might want to.*

"Why not? You've got good taste. I never would have thought of making this room dark green, but I like it."

"Paint's relatively easy to replace, but furniture is another thing entirely."

Caleb looked as if he'd like to argue the point.

Sabrina thought better of pursuing the topic; for a man who changed girlfriends nearly as often as he changed neckties, replacing a room full of furniture might not be as big a deal as she assumed. "I still think it would save a lot of trouble if you just called the Pinnacle and booked a private room."

"Jennings would be hurt if I backed out after all the effort he's gone to."

And what about my effort? Sabrina fumed, but she went straight on. "Then there would be no rented furniture, no rented rug, no need to worry about a spilled glass of red wine.... You know, I haven't even begun to think of what I'm going to do for china. What little you've got is more like pottery, and the pieces don't even match."

"Borrow some from Cassie. Brides always have stuff like that coming out their ears."

She stared at him in disbelief. "Before she's even married, much less before she's had a chance to use it herself? You are joking, aren't you?"

"Why are women always so sentimental about things

like plates?'' Caleb asked plaintively. ''You'd think I was asking to go along on the honeymoon.''

''Believe me, a honeymoon is the last thing I'd expect you to want to join!''

Caleb grinned. ''Well, now that you mention it, you're probably right. Anyway, if you're too sensitive to borrow dishes, go buy some.''

The mere thought of being seen wandering through the china department choosing patterns made Sabrina shudder. The rumors would really fly then. ''I'll figure something out. Is there anything else I should know about your guest before the party?''

Caleb shrugged. ''I don't know that much about him myself. What do you want to know?''

''It would be really helpful to know if he's allergic to any foods, and also how much of a stickler he is on etiquette rules. At the moment, it looks as if there will only be seven of us—I'm short a woman guest. I could twist Paige's arm and make her fill in, but she really doesn't want to come. However, if not having a dinner partner is likely to bother Austin Weaver—''

''If that sort of detail is likely to bother him, I don't think he'll fit in real well at Tanner.''

''Now that you mention it,'' Sabrina said crisply, ''you're absolutely right.''

Caleb shot a suspicious look at her. ''If you're implying that my etiquette is a little rusty, Sabrina—''

''Not exactly. But the last time I looked up blackmail in my Emily Post, she still frowned on it.''

''Here I thought you were talking about the rule against living together. But as long as it's only blackmail that you're objecting to, there's no reason why—''

''If you're building up to suggesting that I go to bed with you, Caleb—''

"I'm not building up to it," Caleb said. "I'm already there."

"Then let me remind you of why you said you've never had anybody living with you before. You explained it all very patiently—because it's so much easier to invite them in than it is to invite them to leave."

"But the same rules don't apply to you," he declared.

"I'm one of a kind, all right," Sabrina said wearily. "Look, I've had a really long day and I'm not in the mood to spar about it any more. I know the plan was for you to go upstairs to your own bed tonight, but after that fall you took... I mean, it would only take a minute to clear off the hospital bed, and then you wouldn't have—"

"The space to invite you to join me," Caleb said.

"I was thinking about having the stairs to climb."

"I see." He sounded faintly disappointed. "No, the paint fumes down here are too strong to handle. I can drag myself up to my room. Of course, I wouldn't want you to be too far away, in case I need you. For anything at all."

"Careful," Sabrina warned, "or I'll confiscate your crutches and you'll be stranded altogether."

He laughed and leaned on her as he hopped up the steps.

One of a kind, she thought as she settled on the air mattress, once more on the floor in the almost-empty room across the hall from the master bedroom. Where Caleb was concerned, she was without doubt the exception that proved all the rules.

And she should be glad he thought of her that way, Sabrina told herself firmly. Not only as one of a kind—but definitely not *his* kind.

A leg immobilizer and a set of crutches were not apt to catch on as classy fashion accessories, Caleb thought as Jennings tightened the immobilizer's straps over what until then had been a perfect trouser crease. "Just help me with the shoe I can't reach," he said, "and then you'd better get back downstairs before the guests start arriving."

"Miss Saunders is somewhat anxious, sir," Jennings admitted.

About to go into orbit was a better way to put it, Caleb thought. Sabrina had been acting all day as if they were entertaining royalty tonight—or maybe her future parents-in-law. He frowned, wondering what had put that particular image into his mind. All that talk about bridal china and honeymoons last night?

Caleb slid into his jacket, straightened his tie and paused at the top of the stairs to send one crutch scooting down so it would be waiting for him. Then he braced himself between the banister and his remaining crutch so he could hop down one slow step at a time.

In the dining room, with her back to the door, Sabrina was lighting the tall tapered candles nestled in the floral centerpiece. Caleb leaned on his crutches and watched, admiring the simple lines of her figure-hugging white sheath.

"Beautiful," he said, and was surprised at the way his voice caught.

Sabrina glanced over her shoulder, frowning. Caleb wondered what she was deducing from that odd crack in his voice and decided it would be prudent not to give her a chance to think about it—heaven only knew what wild ideas she'd conjure up.

"The table," he said improvising. "It's beautiful. I knew you could come up with the goods."

The little frown between her eyebrows eased. "It's Paige's china," she said. "I can still hardly believe it."

Caleb was puzzled. Plates were plates, weren't they? He looked more closely at the nearest place setting and took a guess. "You mean the color?"

"Well, the trim on the china *is* a perfect match for the color of the walls, but that's not really what I was talking about. I meant I can hardly believe that she owns it at all."

He was thoroughly at sea. "Why shouldn't she have china?"

Sabrina sighed. "I can't even explain. It's just not like Paige—our practical Paige—to own something that's so very bridal. And it's not like it's been passed down in the family, either—they've only been making this pattern for a few years."

Caleb shrugged. "So she likes nice dishes."

"But she never uses them. In fact, they were packed away in the attic."

He struck a pose, as best he could considering the crutches, lowered his voice and pretended to be an old-time radio announcer. "Don't touch that dial. Stay tuned for The Mystery of the Reappearing Plates, starring—"

Sabrina laughed, but she shook her head as if confused. "All right, it obviously sounds like I'm making a big deal out of nothing. But you don't know Paige very well, or you'd realize—"

Caleb leaned one crutch against the back of a chair and cupped his palm under her chin. "I realize that you're driving yourself nuts with details."

"Somebody's got to, if the party's going to be a success."

"But now it's time to let them go," he said softly, "and enjoy yourself."

Her breath was coming fast, and just as he bent to kiss her, she caught her lower lip between even white teeth and whispered, "Not now."

He wondered if she realized how much that sounded like a promise. Whether she'd said it deliberately or it was some sort of Freudian slip didn't matter, however, for the message was pretty much the same. He'd still have to play his cards carefully, but in some indefinable way the rules of the game had changed in the space of the last few minutes. And he knew he was going to win.

But the prospect of victory wasn't enough to satisfy him right now. The taste of her, on the other hand—

"Jennings will be needing help," she said hastily.

Caleb didn't bother to answer. But just as his mouth brushed hers, the doorbell wheezed.

Sabrina pulled away. "That will be your guest," she said. "There's so much still that I have to do...but you'd like to have a few minutes alone with him anyway, wouldn't you?"

"Not as much as I'd like to have a few minutes alone with you," Caleb muttered. But she was already gone, toward the safety of the kitchen. He sighed and tried to re-align his thoughts. Moving from seduction to job interview in the space of a few seconds was a strain not only on the brain but on the body, as well.

The man on the doorstep was not quite what Caleb had expected, but he couldn't immediately put his finger on where the difference lay. He knew, however, that it wasn't physical. Austin Weaver was as close as anyone ever looked to his publicity photos—his black hair and gray eyes had reproduced beautifully in the magazine's glossy pages, and Caleb would have recognized him anywhere. He was dressed exactly as Caleb had expected he would be, in the standard executive costume—custom-fitted charcoal suit, perfect haircut, wing-tip shoes. So what made him different?

"Glad you can join us," Caleb said. "Come in." He juggled his crutches so he could shake hands, then led the way into the living room, where Jennings had set up a bar tray on the coffee table. "I can pour you a drink, but as you can see you'll have to carry it yourself.'' He eased onto the edge of the couch.

"Scotch and water,'' Austin Weaver said. "Easy on the Scotch. It's a little early in the season for a skiing accident, isn't it?''

"Haven't even been on a slope yet, and it doesn't look like I'll make it anytime soon, either. I did this at a children's Halloween party.'' Caleb handed over the glass and fixed one for himself.

Austin stirred his drink. "You have children?''

"No, the party was for my employees' kids. One of the ways a small company can stand out. We're making a real push at creating a family-friendly atmosphere to help us keep good employees.''

"Good idea.''

"You'll see some of that in action tomorrow—at least, I'm assuming you'll have time to stop by to take a look at the business.'' *Don't sound too eager,* Caleb warned himself.

"My flight isn't till noon. And I always like seeing what's going on in the business world.''

And that, Caleb thought, was the best nonanswer he'd heard all day. Of course, that was the way the negotiations game was played.

Sabrina came in, carrying a crystal tray full of hot hors d'oeuvres.

Austin Weaver was on his feet before his host could even reach for his crutches. Caleb was vaguely annoyed; rising when a lady entered the room was one thing, he thought, but this guy had jumped up as if he'd gotten an electrical shock.

He glanced at Sabrina and thought better of his assessment. Maybe Austin Weaver *had* gotten a shock; most men, when they first met Sabrina Saunders, would probably be

just as stunned. He might have reacted the same way himself—except that on his first encounter with her he'd been
in too much pain to dwell on her attributes, and ever since
then the lingering memory had helped keep his senses in
line.

She really was gorgeous, Caleb admitted. Add the way
that slim white dress hugged her in all the right places, and
he could understand the way Austin Weaver was acting.
Still, he felt like nudging the guy and telling him to quit
panting and reel in his tongue.

"Mrs. Tanner?" Austin Weaver asked.

From where Caleb was sitting, he couldn't see Sabrina's
expression, but he could tell that her eyelashes dropped—
modestly, no doubt—and from the curve of her cheek he
knew she was smiling just a little. "Not quite," she murmured. "Well, actually, not even close."

She's flirting, Caleb thought in astonishment. What had
gotten into the woman? Was she so attracted to Austin
Weaver that she'd forgotten the part she was supposed to
be playing? He cleared his throat.

Sabrina looked at him blankly, as if she'd forgotten he
was there. "Oh, would you like a cheese puff, Caleb?" she
asked sweetly and offered him the tray. Then she set it
aside, perched on a chair next to Austin Weaver and asked
him about his trip.

He heard the doorbell and considered levering himself
up to answer it—heaven knew Sabrina was too absorbed to
notice that asthmatic wheeze—until he heard Jennings
crossing the hall. A moment later, the living room seemed
to be full of people. Jake and Cassie, apologizing for being
late. Right behind them was the production manager and
his date....

Except the woman standing beside the engineer wasn't

the brainless doll who was usually on his arm. Instead, he was escorting Angelique.

Aggravation chewed at Caleb. What was Sabrina thinking of, he fumed, to invite *her?* Was this some misguided effort to illustrate the contrast between the two of them? She had a lot to learn if she thought she could get by with that kind of game!

"Hello, Caleb," Angelique said, almost purring. "You're looking..." She let the sentence trail off, as if she couldn't bring herself to say what she really believed because it would be unflattering but nevertheless refused to lie about it. "Sabrina, darling." She kissed the air beside Sabrina's cheek. "I hope you don't mind me stepping into your party at the last moment."

Caleb's annoyance level dropped a fraction as he realized that Sabrina looked just as shell-shocked as he felt.

Angelique went straight on in her low drawl. "My friend Missa had a migraine tonight. She was going to force herself to come anyway, because she just hated the thought of disappointing you and upsetting your table seating, but I told her I'd take her place." Her smile looked more like a grimace. "The poor darling was so relieved to be able to stay home." She blinked. "Oh—well, of course I didn't mean it to sound *that* way."

Yes, you did, Caleb thought. *What did I ever see in this woman?*

Angelique looked around. "Is this everyone? You mean we're only seven for dinner, after all? What a pity, Sabrina dear, that you don't have an extra female friend. You should have asked—I'd have been happy to introduce you to some of mine. But of course I can see why you wouldn't want to risk the competition."

From the corner of his eye, Caleb saw a flutter of fabric in the hallway, and his mother stepped into the room. "Or possibly," Catherine Tanner said, "she didn't want to risk the boredom. Jennings tells me dinner is served, Sabrina dear."

Caleb shut his mouth with a snap. He wasn't in the habit of experiencing premonitions, but it seemed he'd hit this one on the head when he'd been speculating that Sabrina was fussing as much as if she was entertaining her future in-laws.

Catherine was watching him, he noted. "If you're wondering why I'm here," she murmured, "it's because Sabrina called and asked for my help. What else would family do?"

He'd deal with that complication later, Caleb decided as he hoisted himself from the couch. "Sorry I can't exactly offer you my arm, Sabrina—"

Too late, he realized that she was holding out a hand to Austin Weaver, instead.

Beside him, his mother murmured, "Wipe that frown off your face, Caleb—this is supposed to be a party. And don't argue, either. Since I am the senior woman present—much as I hate to admit it—you're to have the pleasure of taking me in to dinner, while your hostess quite correctly devotes herself to the guest of honor." She patted his arm. "Don't they make a cute couple? Both so dark and so handsome. Caleb, dear, don't grind your teeth like that. Surely you don't think you could monopolize Sabrina at a dinner party?"

Of course I don't, Caleb thought. *Come to that, why would I even want to?*

CHAPTER EIGHT

SABRINA settled into her place at the foot of the dining table and smiled her thanks at Austin Weaver for pushing in her chair. Her lips felt stiff and dry, and there was a dull, throbbing ache at her temples. The evening had scarcely begun, and already it was threatening to become an unmitigated disaster.

Of all the people who could have shown up to take an absent guest's place—and of all nights for a substitution—it would have to be Angelique. Sabrina wondered what kind of bribe the woman had offered her so-called friend to produce that probably specious migraine.

And Caleb wasn't helping matters any. Couldn't he see that glowering like a thundercloud wasn't going to suppress Angelique? In fact, it was only egging her on, encouraging her to get even more outrageous.

Meanwhile, Austin Weaver was getting the wrong idea altogether—of the gathering, of Caleb, of Tanner Electronics as a whole. It wouldn't surprise Sabrina a bit if the man bolted from the dining room straight to the airport and chartered a plane to take him home instead of waiting for his commercial flight tomorrow.

She glanced around the table, noted that everyone was seated, and nodded to Jennings to begin serving the soup.

Next to her, she saw Austin Weaver's tanned hand reaching for his napkin, and she heard him take a long, deep breath. It sounded like a sigh in reverse.

He's bracing himself for the ordeal, she thought. And yet it hadn't sounded like that kind of reaction. It hadn't been resigned or determined. He'd sounded almost startled, as if he'd seen something he hadn't expected to see.

Puzzled, she turned to look at him. He was staring at something on the table, she thought. A chipped plate, maybe? Though she really couldn't imagine a detail like that causing him to react so strongly; a man who didn't turn a hair during a scene like Angelique had made would hardly get upset about faulty china. Besides, Sabrina reminded herself, she'd carefully inspected every piece herself as she'd set the table just a couple of hours ago.

So what *had* he seen that had startled him? She hoped it wasn't an insect in the centerpiece.

He intercepted her look and smiled. "I was just noticing what a pretty table you've set."

Sabrina didn't buy that for a minute, but she didn't have much choice except to play along. "Thank you. Food always tastes so much better when it's served well, I think."

"Are these family pieces?" He touched a fingertip to a fine-stemmed wineglass.

"Some of them. The crystal and flatware belong to Catherine, actually—Caleb's mother, that is. She had them even before he was born."

"How nice of her to pass the things along so you can enjoy them now."

Something like that, Sabrina thought, remembering the cartons stacked in the sunroom, waiting to haul Catherine's crystal back to Boulder the moment the party was over.

The table had gone quiet except for the soft clink of a soup ladle in the tureen that Jennings was offering to each guest in turn. It was apparent that Angelique had heard the comment, for she sent a look at Sabrina that should have turned her into charcoal. Sabrina wondered if the dislike in Angelique's gaze was on general principle, or if she'd coveted Catherine's belongings.

Catherine had obviously heard the remark, too. She looked directly at Angelique as she said, "I think it is such a blessing, Mr. Weaver, that Caleb's finally found a woman who truly appreciates my pretty things."

Angelique narrowed her eyes venomously.

Caleb shrugged. "Personally, I think it's just easier to drink out of the milk carton."

"See what I mean?" Catherine murmured.

Sabrina suppressed a shudder. Things were rapidly going from bad to worse. "Are you a collector of china and glassware, Mr. Weaver? Antiques, perhaps?"

He smiled. "Oh, no. At our house we're much more likely to use paper plates. They're microwave safe, you know."

Sabrina felt a little deflated. Maybe it wasn't fair, but she'd expected a bit more class from someone in Austin Weaver's position.

Though why shouldn't the man use disposable dishes? she asked herself. *He's hardly likely to want champagne and caviar three times a day.*

"Well, not every meal can be a banquet, I suppose." Sabrina stole a look at his left hand. No wedding ring—but he'd said *our,* hadn't he? "The lady in your life didn't accompany you on this trip? What a shame that she didn't see you get your award."

Austin shook his head. "She would have hated missing the preschool visit to the zoo."

Sabrina wondered for an instant if she'd heard right. Of course, there was no reason the woman shouldn't teach in a preschool. Not every wife of a powerful executive was a mindless doll, and at least this woman was accomplishing something worthwhile instead of spending time on manicures and massages.

"I should explain, obviously," Austin said. "My daugh-

ter, Jennifer, is five years old. There are just the two of
us.''

Sabrina was almost sorry to discover that the woman
she'd been picturing was only a figment of her imagination,
after all. The fictional Mrs. Weaver had sounded like a
possible friend.

Cassie, on Austin's other side, said, "You're a single
parent *and* you hold down a high-powered job?''

"Watch yourself,'' Jake said. "Here comes the sales
pitch.''

Austin looked puzzled.

"You've landed right in the middle of their business,''
Caleb said. "Sabrina and Cassie and their partner, I mean.
They call it Rent-A-Wife—but hey, if you decide to move
to Denver, Austin, maybe you can talk them into expanding
it into Rent-A-Mom.''

Sabrina pretended to ignore him. "We'd be happy to
assist if we can,'' she said. "We don't actually baby-sit,
but we help a lot of working parents keep up with things
like buying school uniforms and making routine trips to the
orthodontist. With us handling the details, moms and dads
can spend more time on the important events. We'd take
good care of you and Jennifer.''

"I must say you make Denver sound very attractive,''
Austin said.

Feeling a flicker of triumph, Sabrina caught Caleb's eye
and was startled at the coolness she saw there. That was
odd, she thought. Surely he hadn't objected to her explain-
ing Rent-A-Wife; he'd practically done it himself.

And shouldn't he be pleased that they were all trying, in
every way possible, to make Austin Weaver feel that a
move to Denver would be a good one for him and his
family?

But the chilliness she'd seen in his eyes seemed to leap

across the table. It stayed with her all through dinner, and it made her bones feel cold.

The party broke up early. Austin Weaver was the first to make a move to leave; after the way the evening had gone, that wouldn't have surprised Sabrina even if he hadn't been the honored guest. What did startle her was the fact that Caleb didn't conveniently forget to renew his invitation for Austin to visit Tanner Electronics in the morning. Instead, he emphasized it—and even more surprising, Austin said he'd be there.

Still puzzled by that exchange, Sabrina stood beside Caleb at the front door to say good-night to the other guests. Maybe, she thought, the two of them were just being extraordinarily diplomatic, going through the motions even though both realized their discussion had no chance of success, neither willing to be the one to draw the line and call a halt to the pretense. But that, too, was surprising; she'd have bet anything that Austin Weaver was no more inclined to waste time than Caleb was. Maybe the answer was that neither of them wanted to publicly admit their negotiations were going nowhere?

She pulled herself back to the waning party just in time to hear Cassie invite Catherine to her wedding on the following Saturday. "I know it's terribly late to be issuing invitations," Cassie said. "But it's not at all formal, just a whole lot of friends getting together to wish us well. And since you're a brand-new friend, we'd love to have you come if you can."

Angelique, standing nearby, said, "A casual wedding— how charming. It sounds sort of like a spur-of-the-moment picnic. I wouldn't miss it for the world, myself." She was looking straight at Sabrina as she said it.

One more complication, Sabrina thought. One more thing she hadn't considered till this moment.

Informal though the ceremony would be, Cassie's invitations had gone out right on time, a full month before the chosen date. Since Caleb was invited, and since he and Angelique had still been a combination then, she'd necessarily received an invitation, as well. Sabrina vaguely remembered addressing it, in fact, on a long Sunday afternoon when all three of the partners had ended up with writer's cramp as well as stacks of stamped envelopes.

Who could have dreamed that things would change so much in a few short weeks? Angelique's demise might have been predicted, of course; Caleb's record was pretty clear where bimbos were concerned, and that had been only a matter of time. But as for Sabrina's taking her place—

If I'd seen it myself in a crystal ball, Sabrina thought, *I'd have sent the ball out to be polished.*

And of course she hadn't taken Angelique's place, Sabrina reminded herself. This was all show, all performance, with no substance underneath. Which made it even more difficult to understand why Caleb had been so touchy tonight when she'd only been playing her part.

Angelique's voice was low, pitched for only Sabrina to hear. "If I were you, I wouldn't count Catherine's treasures too early. You'll never manage to hang on to Caleb. He's unhappy already—or hadn't you noticed?"

Angelique didn't wait for an answer, which was just as well since Sabrina didn't have one. *Unhappy* was a mild way of describing the way Caleb looked, she thought.

Finally, only Caleb, Sabrina and Catherine were left. Sabrina closed the front door behind the last guest and said, "I'm glad that's over."

"Oh, really?" Caleb's voice was taut. "You could have

fooled me. You seemed to be thoroughly enjoying your-self."

Catherine said, almost too casually, "I think I'll go lend a hand in the kitchen. Paige looked pretty flustered last time I caught a glimpse of her."

Momentarily, Sabrina was distracted. Paige, flustered? That didn't sound like her partner—especially since, from the kitchen side, the party had gone off just beautifully. Musing, she brushed past Caleb and went into the dining room.

"Where do you think you're going?" he growled.

"To finish clearing the table," she said without looking at him. "If you want to talk to me, Caleb, you can follow me around, but I'm not going to stand here for a lecture like a kid who's been called to the principal's office."

"Feeling defensive, I see."

"What? Of course I'm not—if I was, I'd be defending myself." She picked up a tray from the sideboard and be-gan loading it with dessert plates. "However, there's no point in even trying, when I don't have a hint what you think I should be defending myself against. The only thing I can imagine that might have been remotely responsible for setting you off tonight was the sales pitch for Rent-A-Wife, and you started that yourself with the business about Rent-A-Mom. Caleb, for heaven's sake—"

"Is that what you call that little discussion? A sales pitch for Rent-A-Wife?"

"Well, not a first-class one," Sabrina admitted with a smile. "If she'd really been in top form, Cassie would have whipped out a business card, a promotional pamphlet and a contract for services for Austin to review."

Caleb didn't seem to see the humor. "I thought it was just another excuse for you to flirt with Austin Weaver. 'We'll take good care of you and Jennifer,'" he mimicked.

"Dammit, Sabrina, I invited him here for business reasons. It was not in the plan for you to distract him."

Sabrina set a coffee cup onto the tray with a bang. "I was not flirting, I was trying to put the man at ease. And as for distractions—all things considered, I think you should be grateful I was trying to distract him from things like the cat at the other end of the table by telling him the advantages of living in Denver. For you to blame *me* for the evening going badly is the outside of enough, Caleb! All you did was sit there glowering."

"If you expect a medal for martyrdom—"

"I'd rather have combat pay. I earned it. Of course, if you're not happy with the job I'm doing, I'll be quite pleased to go back to my regular schedule starting tomorrow. Now, either make yourself useful or get out of my way." She gathered the delicate brandy snifters into a cluster and balanced two of them atop the pile of dessert plates.

Caleb cleared his throat. "Did my mother really hand over all those wineglasses?"

"She lent them to me. And you should be grateful."

"Grateful for what? Don't let a simple loan give you any ideas, Sabrina."

Sabrina plunged straight on, heedless of the interruption. "Grateful it's only a loan, because if this crystal wasn't hers—and older than you are—I'd be breaking it over your hard head one stem after another." She picked up the tray and sidestepped him on her way to the kitchen.

Jennings was sorting flatware, Paige's rubber-gloved hands were immersed in soapy water, and Catherine was wielding a dish towel while she rehashed the dinner party. She stopped in mid-sentence as Sabrina came in.

"Don't be self-conscious," Sabrina said. "Whatever you have to say about that so-called party can't be any harsher than what I'm thinking."

"It's not that, exactly," Catherine drawled. "I wasn't telling Paige anything I wouldn't say in front of you. I was just wondering if Caleb was finished with his little fit of possessiveness, or if you were simply taking a breather from listening to him."

Sabrina was speechless. *Possessiveness?* Well, she supposed it could have looked that way to an outsider—but she wouldn't have expected that reaction from Catherine, of all people. Catherine, sharp-eyed and cynical, who might not know the details but who clearly understood that something about her son's so-called relationship was wildly off-kilter.

Before Sabrina could find her voice, Caleb said flatly, "I'm finished. You can relax, Mother."

Sabrina jumped at the sound of his voice.

Caleb swung himself into the kitchen. "But I still want to know how Sabrina expects me to be useful when I have both hands occupied with crutches."

Sabrina pointed to the sunroom. "Sit down over there and put the stemware back in the boxes after it's washed, so your mother can take it home."

There, Sabrina thought. *I can't make it any plainer that this simple loan hasn't given me any ideas at all.*

As for whatever ideas were in Caleb's head, however—well, she had no control over those.

What in the dickens was the matter with him? Caleb asked himself as he mechanically slid wineglasses into their slots. So what if she'd flirted a little? He'd have been more irritable if Sabrina had been rude to Austin Weaver or ignored him completely. She'd been doing what any good hostess would have done, that was all.

And doing it entirely too well, a little voice in the back of his mind whispered.

Caleb knew better than to think a man like Austin Weaver would sign on for a new job solely as a way to get to know a particular woman. But if the job intrigued him, the woman might well be the deciding factor....

So why was he annoyed at the idea, when in fact anything that inspired Austin Weaver to consider relocating to Denver would be to Caleb's benefit—and to Tanner Electronics', as well?

By the time Weaver could make a move, Caleb's knee would be fully healed and the reason for this masquerade would be done with. Sabrina would be free to do whatever she liked, and why shouldn't she take up with Austin Weaver if she wanted?

It wasn't as if Caleb wanted to keep her around for himself...was it?

No, he assured himself hastily. On the whole, skydiving and ski jumping and motorcycle racing were exhilarating enough for his taste. Pastimes like Sabrina Saunders were far too risky for his comfort zone, at least in the long run.

Austin Weaver didn't have a clue what he would be letting himself in for if he started toying with Sabrina. But then, that wasn't Caleb's problem. Was it?

The deli where the partners met for lunch every Wednesday wasn't as busy as usual when Sabrina arrived. She ordered her sandwich and carried it over to join Paige, who was seated in the small dining area.

Sabrina added sweetener to her iced tea and unwrapped her turkey on rye. "I can't thank you enough for helping last night, Paige. What would we have done without you—"

Paige shrugged. "You'd have been there for me." She stirred her salad and put her fork down.

"Is that all you're eating?" Sabrina asked. "Or should I say, not eating?"

Cassie came up behind her, putting an arm around Sabrina's shoulders. "I'm glad to see you survived your baptism of fire. First business dinner party with your future mother-in-law attending..."

Sabrina drew a breath to correct her. *She's not my future mother-in-law, and she's never going to be.*

But Cassie hadn't paused. "You know, I didn't even think about how tricky that combination was till after it was all over. You were marvelous, Sabrina. And the food— Paige, it was wonderful." She unloaded a cup of yogurt and a bagel from her tray and sat down.

"Don't give me credit." Paige sorted out a sliver of ham from her lettuce. "I was just the scullery maid. The food was Jennings's department."

She sounded almost wistful, Sabrina thought, as if—too late—she'd regretted her choice to help in the kitchen instead of joining the party in Catherine's place. But it would be tactless to point that out, so Sabrina changed the subject. "The two of you make me feel like a glutton. Of course, you could both eat last night, while I can't even tell you what was on my plate. Besides, I've been cleaning closets for one of our clients all morning, and I'm ravenous."

"Closets?" Cassie said. "You mean Caleb stopped being possessive long enough to let you do some real Rent-A-Wife work?"

There was that word again, Sabrina thought. Odd, that both Catherine and Cassie had used it. "I dropped him off at the office this morning, and Jake's going to take him home. I told him I didn't think it was necessary for me to follow him around any longer when we've got clients who are desperate for help." *Or something like that,* she thought.

"Hear, hear," Paige muttered.

"Sorry," Cassie said. "I shouldn't tease you. But if you've been headfirst in a closet, you obviously don't know anything about how Austin Weaver's tour went this morning."

Sabrina shook her head. "Do you?"

"Not much, just that Jake said he had a lot of questions and everybody got along very well. Now that he's met him, Jake thinks Austin would be a great fit for Tanner."

Paige had picked up her fork to stab at a cherry tomato. The tines slipped, and the tomato shot off her plate and bounced on the tile floor.

"They should cut those things in half before serving them," Cassie said sympathetically. "Otherwise, it's like trying to spear a rubber ball."

"And what does Caleb think?" Sabrina asked.

Cassie looked surprised. "He made Austin an offer. Didn't you think he would?"

Sabrina shrugged. "Nothing would surprise me."

"The big question, of course, is whether Austin Weaver is even interested—but I'm guessing it's unlikely."

"Any particular reason?" Paige idly stirred her salad.

"Because Jake told me Austin just said he'd think it over. If he was serious, surely he'd have tried to get Caleb to better his opening offer."

"Maybe he's reserving that move for later negotiations," Sabrina said.

"Or maybe he knows Caleb can't possibly meet his demands, so there's no point in listing them all." Paige's tone was thoughtful.

"No matter what the reason," Sabrina said wearily, "I suppose in the meantime I'll have to do dinner parties for the other two finalists."

"I'll be out of town that day," Paige announced.

Sabrina stared at her. "But I don't even know what week they'll be, Paige, much less what day. You won't really desert me, will you? There can't be another party like last night, anyway."

"It was one of a kind," Cassie agreed. "Though I don't know what you're fussing about, Paige—you didn't have to listen to Angelique all evening. I was surprised at Austin, though. Weren't you, Sabrina? A nationally famous executive who doesn't have an overwhelming ego—that came as quite a surprise."

Paige pushed her plate away with a jerky movement. "I've got a long list of jobs for this afternoon, so if there isn't any Rent-A-Wife business to discuss—"

"Rent-A-Wife?" Cassie murmured. "I'd almost forgotten that."

"Just how we're going to handle things next week," Sabrina said, "with Cassie gone on her honeymoon. But with Caleb healing, I should be back up to speed."

"You two and your men," Paige said. "It's getting to be just one distraction after another."

Cassie grinned. "And what a distraction," she agreed. "But never mind, Paige, your turn's probably just around the corner."

"Not if I see it coming," Paige muttered.

How quickly habits formed, Sabrina thought with a hint of surprise when she found herself in the driveway in front of Caleb's house late Friday afternoon. Last week, her automatic pilot would have taken her car straight to her condo complex. This week... Now that was a scary thought.

As she detoured to the kitchen to get a glass of ice water, she heard Jennings on the telephone. "I'm sorry, Mr. Maxwell," he was saying as she came in, "but it's impossible."

She couldn't stop herself. "Jennings, if that's Mason Maxwell, I'm sure Caleb will want to talk to him. Caleb's here, isn't he? He must be—we're going to the wedding rehearsal together this evening."

"I would much prefer not to disturb Mr. Tanner this afternoon," Jennings said politely. "In any case, Miss Saunders, since you're here—the gentleman also asked about you." He put the telephone into her hand.

Sabrina would have liked to bite her tongue off, but it was too late. She could already hear the interest in Mason's voice as he asked, "Whose wedding rehearsal?"

"Not mine," she said crisply "Does that please you?"

"Let's just say I'm not surprised. You might like to know that your parents are quite impressed with you, Sabrina—taking up with Caleb Tanner."

"Just couldn't wait to tell them, could you?"

"Your father was so delighted, in fact, that he actually hurt my feelings."

"Because he thinks Caleb is a better catch than you? You ought to know by now that my father isn't oversupplied with tact, Mason. Or judgment, either."

"You could be right. He said something about calling up Caleb to ask his intentions toward you. Of course, when he hears the answer—"

"That warm family approval will feel more like January in the Arctic Circle," Sabrina agreed.

"And I wanted you to know that when your current situation changes, as of course it's bound to, my offer's still open. By then it may be the only way you'll ever patch things up with your parents."

"Mason," she said honestly, "you leave me speechless."

"By the way," Mason said crisply, "as long as I have

you on the phone, ask Caleb how long he plans to keep my candidate hanging while she waits for an interview.''

''Careful,'' Sabrina warned. ''You actually sound as if you think I'm capable of getting a message straight.''

''And tell him not to be surprised, by the time Austin Weaver gets around to turning him down, if my candidate has already taken another job.''

The telephone clicked against Sabrina's ear. She put it down and slowly climbed the stairs.

The door of Caleb's bedroom stood open, but no one was inside. The bathroom was steamy and smelled of his soap, but it, too, was empty. She was turning toward the small guest room to change her clothes for the rehearsal when she saw that the attic stairway was open, and she heard a rhythmic rattle coming from the third floor.

No wonder Jennings hadn't wanted to disturb him, she thought. Caleb was up there playing with his trains.

From the top of the stairs, she could see him sitting on a tall stool, watching intently as a scale-model freight train made its way across a platform built all the way around the perimeter of the single huge room. For a moment, Sabrina thought he hadn't heard her, but he flipped a switch on the control panel in front of him, the train halted, and he shifted on the stool till he was facing her.

His eyes were gleaming with enthusiasm, and Sabrina felt a little flutter deep inside. She told herself not to be ridiculous. It was only the trains that had put that brightness in his eyes, and the fact that he was mobile enough to enjoy them again. That was all.

She looked away, studying the room as if she was seeing it for the first time. Once a ballroom, it still retained traces of its early grandeur, with carved moldings and gilt trim and a crystal chandelier.

''I suppose you're going to make me leave my toys,''

Caleb grumbled. "After all the work it took to get up here, too."

"You're obviously feeling better, to climb all those stairs."

"Only one crutch today. I thought I'd try it out—I wouldn't be much good as an usher at the wedding tomorrow if I needed them both." He pushed himself off the stool.

He wasn't going to need crutches at all much longer, Sabrina thought. Or her following him around to help, either.

What should have been a comforting realization somehow left a hollow feeling deep inside her. *It's just gotten to be a habit,* she told herself firmly. *That's all. You'll get over it.*

Caleb peered around her. "What have you got behind your back?"

"Funny you should ask. I was thinking the same thing— about the crutches, I mean." She held out the stick she carried. "I found it in an antique shop this morning while I was waiting for the dealer to set a value on a client's vase. I thought it would be the perfect touch of elegance at the wedding."

The cane was almost black—made of teak or ebony, she thought—and the surface gleamed not with varnish but with the friction of long handling. Caleb's hand closed over the polished knob at the top. "You know," he said, "if it hadn't been for that damned helium tank at the Halloween party, we might just be meeting for the first time at the rehearsal tonight."

She looked at him in astonishment. Caleb, sounding positively sentimental? What had gotten into him? "It would have been a lot nicer for you that way," she admitted. "You wouldn't have needed the cane."

Caleb looked thoughtful. "I'm not so sure. If we'd met under those circumstances, with you on your best behavior, I might have just thought of you as a beautiful woman."

Sabrina's heart turned over with sudden longing. How she would like to go back and change that single episode, she admitted. But not just to escape the difficulties of the past week. Not to avoid Caleb.

We could have had a clean start instead, she thought. It could have all been so different. Without the pain and wariness and resentment that her clumsiness had caused, anything might have happened....

Caleb smiled. "And I might not have realized you weren't just gorgeous, you were deadly, too."

Sabrina hardly heard him. *Anything might have happened,* she was thinking. *He might even have come to love me, just as I love him....*

CHAPTER NINE

NO SOONER had the thought scorched across her mind than Sabrina tried to tell herself it wasn't possible. It was as if that odd sentimental note in Caleb's voice had been contagious, she told herself. For a moment, he'd sounded almost wistful—and a darned good piece of acting it had been, too, setting her up for the punch line like that—and the tinge of sentimentality had leaped like wildfire from him to her.

It had thrown her, that was all. Startled her. Caused a sort of electrical misfire in her brain.

But that screwball thought didn't mean she'd fallen for him. Nothing of the kind.

She certainly wasn't in *love* with the man.

She could hardly bring herself to enunciate the word, even in her mind, because the whole concept was so chilling. She didn't even *like* Caleb Tanner, so how could she possibly—

But that wasn't quite the truth, she admitted. She did like him. She'd grown to like him rather a lot, once she'd gotten to know him. But that was a whole continent away from loving him. She had a good deal more sense than to let herself do that.

Just as any other woman would, she felt the power of his personal attraction—Sabrina would admit to that much. But fall in love with Caleb Tanner? Not even the bimbo contingent was that foolish. Sabrina would bet her last dollar that Angelique had never suffered a moment's illusion

151

about being in love with him. His bank book, maybe, but not Caleb himself.

So if even the bimbos knew better, then Sabrina—educated, intelligent, experienced Sabrina—couldn't possibly have gone overboard. It was unthinkable. Not even to be considered.

So why are you still thinking about it? asked her conscience. *If it's such a stupid idea, why haven't you just put it out of your mind?*

Caleb was looking at her oddly, his head tipped to one side, as if he was wondering why his teasing comment seemed to have struck a nerve.

Sabrina forced herself to smile and play along. "Lucky for you I wasn't up to my full potential that day, or you wouldn't be out of the hospital yet. Of course, it would have been a good excuse to miss the wedding."

"Why does everybody assume I'm against weddings?" Caleb said plaintively. "I enjoy them the same way I do major-league football—from the sidelines."

"But put you down on the field in the midst of the action—"

"And I'll take to my heels," he agreed. "When the odds are overwhelming that you'll be battered into hamburger, it's not courageous to stand firm, it's pure idiocy."

"Maybe you should put that philosophy down in writing and give it to every woman in your life as sort of an employee handbook. It would save everybody trouble in the long run." Sabrina glanced at her watch. "How long is it going to take you to get back downstairs? If it's longer than five minutes, you'd better start now, while I go change clothes."

"Wait just a minute." Caleb leaned forward to turn the switch that started the train running once more. The freight cars rocked along the track, around the ballroom and straight toward her.

Sabrina watched, almost hypnotized by the rhythm, till the train slowed and halted directly in front of her. In one of the hopper cars, the sort that in real life would carry coal or grain, lay a long, flat package wrapped in silver paper.

Caleb said softly, "That's just a little thank-you for handling the dinner party the other night."

Tentatively, she picked up the package. The paper felt slick against her fingertips. Inside the box, on a bed of cotton, lay a slim platinum bracelet. It was simple, elegant and precisely to her taste; Caleb couldn't have chosen better if he'd read her mind. In fact, it was so perfect that Sabrina wanted to cry, because it seemed to stand for what could have been....

No, she told herself firmly. *You're not supposed to think about that any more. Remember? You're not really in love with him. That thought was a flash of madness.*

He'd made a sweet but casual gesture—and treating this gift as anything more would only lead to uncomfortable questions. She held the bracelet up, turning it to watch the engraving on the flat links catch the light from the chandelier. "Pretty," she said, keeping her voice as nonchalant as if platinum bracelets were an everyday occurrence. "I bet you buy these by the case so you'll always have them on hand."

Caleb snapped his fingers. "I knew I was forgetting something," he said cheerfully. "Thanks—I'll call the jeweler tomorrow to restock my supply."

Half a dozen people were milling about the back of the small chapel, waiting for the pastor, when Caleb and Sabrina arrived. At least, Caleb thought, this wasn't going to be one of those movie-production weddings where the cast numbered in the hundreds and every movement was choreographed to be letter-perfect and smack on time; Cassie was too sensible and down-to-earth for that.

In fact, Cassie was an altogether nice girl. She didn't exactly set Caleb's bones on fire, but he granted that Jake had made a good choice; if the man felt he had to get married, he could have done a lot worse than to choose a woman like Cassie.

On the other hand, no matter how nice she was, the basic question remained in Caleb's mind. Why *did* the man feel he had to get married? What made Jake so certain that he was doing the right thing and that this was the one and only woman for him?

How did *anybody* know?

For Caleb, of course, it was purely a theoretical question, to be poked at in his spare time but never taken truly seriously. As he'd told Sabrina, he considered weddings in the light of a spectator sport—only slightly more rehearsed than pro wrestling, somewhat less absorbing than championship basketball and no competition at all for the World Cup. In other words, interesting—but hardly something he wanted to go into training for. Still, the problem fascinated him. Of all the people in the world, how did anyone know when they'd found the right one?

The question nagged at him even though it held no personal significance. He'd long ago concluded that there was no right woman for him, no one female for whom he would ever consider settling down. He found the phenomenon of Jake's self-confident absorption in the woman of his dreams not only fascinating but completely foreign. Caleb could not imagine ever being so single-minded, or so certain.

As the pastor gathered them into a group to begin their instructions for the rehearsal, Caleb's gaze fell on Sabrina, directly across the circle.

She was wearing red tonight—deep, rich red silk that looked almost purplish in the subdued light of the chapel. She raised a hand to push a lock of shiny black hair behind her ear, and he saw the gleam of platinum on her wrist and congratulated himself on the choice he'd made.

Gold wouldn't have been right for her at all, but the aristocratic mystery of platinum somehow reminded him of Sabrina herself. Everybody liked gold, but it was obvious, even showy. It took a special appreciation to understand the appeal of platinum. Some people thought it was too cold to be truly beautiful, but Caleb knew better. Though it could look like ice, when it was properly handled platinum stopped being chilly and remote. It would never be ordinary, like gold, for it would always maintain its classic beauty. But underneath, it could be just as fiery and as seductive and as satiny smooth to the touch.

Just as he suspected Sabrina could be. If, of course, she was properly handled....

He'd teased her about going to bed with him. But this was different. His mouth grew dry at the thought of cracking that gorgeously cool exterior and releasing the volcano underneath.

As if she felt him watching her, Sabrina glanced across the circle. Her eyes, shadowed by the dimness of the chapel, looked even bigger than usual. An instant later, her gaze flitted uneasily away.

As if, he thought, she could hold him at bay by simply turning her back and concentrating on something else! In fact, it wasn't a question of whether he'd succeed. Now that he'd made up his mind to make love to her, the only uncertainties were when and precisely how he was going to go about persuading her.

Caleb was staring at her. Sabrina tried not to look at him, tried not to swallow hard, tried not to show by the slightest hint of body language that she was aware of the way he was surveying her—a way that was different from any other time he'd looked at her.

Different, without a doubt. But precisely what had changed? What could account for that difference?

The only thing Sabrina could think of was that crazy flash she'd experienced at the house, that fleeting moment when she'd wondered if perhaps she'd fallen in love with him.

Had he read her mind? Had the notion that she'd succumbed to his charm turned him into an eagle, ready to pounce on his helpless prey?

Surely not, she thought. The idea of a woman being in love with him—seriously in love, as opposed to physically attracted— was one that was more likely to make Caleb Tanner act like a cowering rabbit, running for the nearest safe hole. Desire he was used to. Lust he could handle. Love—well, that was another thing altogether.

And in any case, that flash of hers had been nothing more than a momentary lapse in common sense. It hadn't been real—so he couldn't be reacting to it.

She didn't realize that her gaze had drifted to him until the pastor said, ''And who will have the rings tomorrow?''

She watched as Caleb shifted his cane to his left hand so he could fumble in his pocket for Cassie's wedding ring. The pastor took it and added politely, ''And the groom's?''

Only then did Sabrina realize that she'd been so absorbed in watching Caleb she'd forgotten entirely about Jake's ring. She pulled it off her thumb, almost getting it stuck on her knuckle because of her haste, and handed it over.

Caleb was watching her again. Sabrina expected he'd be amused at her clumsiness, but there was no hint of humor in his eyes. Instead, the intensity of his gaze seemed to chafe her skin, warming it almost to the point of ignition. She could feel the slow rise of heat in her face.

Unable to face the power of his gaze any longer, Sabrina turned her attention to the bridal couple instead. She watched, enthralled, the glow in Cassie's eyes as she looked at Jake while he slid her wedding ring onto her finger.

And this is only the practice run, Sabrina thought. *I wonder what she'll look like tomorrow, when it's the real thing.*

Cassie's whole being was wrapped up in the man she loved. But what made her truly lucky was that he felt precisely the same way about her.

Sabrina thought, *I wish that Caleb—*

She stopped herself short, but it was too late. Though the thought remained incomplete, the knowledge behind it was impossible to repress any longer. The idea of loving Caleb hadn't been the flash of madness she'd tried to convince herself it was. The real madness had lain in trying to deny the reality.

But there was no denying it any longer. She'd danced around the subject as long as she could, but faced with Cassie's example Sabrina could no longer disavow her feelings.

She had fallen in love with Caleb. Not with the tycoon, not with the playboy, but with the man inside—the sometimes vulnerable, sometimes difficult but always entrancing man.

Foreknowledge of his attractiveness had not protected her. Determination not to succumb to his charm had not protected her. Scorn of his life-style had not protected her.

Maybe, she thought, there was nothing that could have protected her against his charisma. Under the circumstances—being thrown into contact with him on a constant basis, feeling at least partly responsible for his pain, trying to ease his discomfort—perhaps nothing would have prevented her from tumbling into love with him. Certainly no other woman had ever seen him in the way Sabrina had; no other woman had ever been so exposed to his magnetism.

She might as well have wrapped herself in aluminum foil and walked into the core of a nuclear reactor; she'd have had just as much chance of coming out unaffected.

What was there about him that negated common sense?

Attraction was a funny thing, able to conceal itself in all kinds of disguises....

Sabrina remembered thinking that, one day when she'd wondered whether Paige was succumbing to Caleb's charm. But she hadn't taken the next logical step and applied that reasoning to herself. She'd simply assumed that she was as immune to him as he certainly was to her. And all the time, too blinded by his charm even to see what was happening to her, she'd been sinking deeper into the quicksand of her love for him.

In fact, she admitted, she had been feeling jealous of Paige that day. The bimbo contingent had never caused Sabrina much discomfort, but she'd been acutely sensitive to the possibility that where a woman like Paige was concerned, Caleb might be attracted in return. Sabrina had been feeling possessive, though she'd managed to hide it from herself under an umbrella of disdain. She'd been afraid that someone might try to take him away from her....

As if, she thought with a trace of contempt for her naive self, it was possible to take away something she'd never had. She had never held a claim on Caleb Tanner, and she never would.

But nobody else was ever going to, either.

Sabrina was contemplating the implications of that spare, harsh thought when she heard a unexpected tremor in Cassie's voice as she practiced her vows. Sabrina instantly saw the reason for her friend's tremulousness. Jake was looking at his bride, his fingertips brushing her cheek and a blaze of possessive pride in his eyes that was, Sabrina thought, next door to indecent. No wonder Cassie's voice was shaky.

If Caleb ever looked at me like that, Sabrina thought, *I'd melt on the spot.*

Of course, there was no danger of that. No matter what she wanted—and Sabrina would admit, if only to herself, that she longed to be as important to Caleb as Cassie was to Jake—fact was fact. There was no point, now that she'd faced the main truth, in trying to dodge the smaller but no less unpalatable ones. What she wanted she could not have.

But that didn't mean she couldn't have anything at all.

She could not have his love, but she could have tenderness and passion. She could not have forever, but she could use the present to store up memories....

She could seduce him. Or allow him to seduce her; it ended up being the same thing.

Almost unwillingly, she looked across the circle, over the clasped hands of the bride and groom, at Caleb. He was leaning on his cane, both hands gripping the knob and helping to provide support and balance.

He seemed to read a message in her gaze, for she saw one dark eyebrow lift ever so slightly. What that meant, Sabrina wasn't certain. Was he intrigued? Exasperated? Cautious?

Had she given herself away? Had he read in her eyes that she was desperately serious about him?

Or had she merely imagined that he'd reacted at all? For after that one long look, he seemed to pay no more attention to her whatever.

Sabrina couldn't decide whether to hope that he'd missed her meaning or that he'd chosen to ignore it. Whichever was the case, the result would be the same—nothing. But the feelings behind it...she wasn't quite sure if she preferred him to be indifferent or actively wary. On the whole, she thought indifference would be worse; it implied that she didn't matter at all....

The rehearsal wound to its conclusion, and the bridal party quickly dispersed to the Pinnacle, just a few blocks away, for the rehearsal dinner.

She retrieved her car from the parking lot down the street from the chapel and waited at the curb for Caleb. As she watched, he slapped Jake playfully on the shoulder and came toward her, his face still alight with laughter.

Obviously, she thought, any question he'd had about her was forgotten. His reaction had been indifference, then—confirming that she didn't matter at all.

Just get through the drive, Sabrina told herself, *and you won't have to be alone with him again for hours.* By then she could reestablish her poise, get her balance back, maybe even forget that absurd idea of seducing him.

"What's so funny?" she asked, her voice carefully casual.

"Jake's brother just asked him if the reason groomsmen so often wear black tuxedos is as a symbol of mourning for their fellow man in his last moments of bachelorhood."

Sabrina shook her head. "I had no idea he was capable of such poetic flights of fancy. I only hope his wife didn't hear him say it."

"No, she was a safe distance away." Caleb chuckled softly. "I got Jake's ring back for you to keep overnight."

"Oh—thanks. I forgot." If he asked why her main duty had slipped her mind, Sabrina thought, she'd just tell him she'd been concerned about him having to stand so long.

But he didn't ask, and in only a couple of minutes she

was turning the car over to the valet at the entrance of the hotel that housed the Pinnacle.

Caleb looked at the top story, which slowly revolved so that every table sooner or later had a perfect view of the Rocky Mountains on the western horizon. "Now's my chance to really give my cane a tryout," he said. "If it works on that uncertain moving floor, I'll know I'm well on the road to recovery."

"You were standing so long, I wouldn't be surprised if your knee is too stiff to let you move easily."

He lifted both eyebrows. "Why, Sabrina—one would think you wanted me to stay an invalid."

Yes, she thought. *Because then you'll need me longer.* She shrugged. "I just don't want you injuring yourself again and blaming me."

"In that case, I'll lean on you very heavily as we get to the revolving section."

He didn't, though; they rode up in the elevator with a group, and he leaned on Jake instead. In fact, Sabrina noted, Caleb hadn't touched her since the start of the rehearsal.

And he didn't touch her all the way through dinner. He didn't make any suggestive remarks, either—and that was even less like Caleb.

Not that he was obvious about it, of course. To the others at the table, his behavior must have appeared perfectly normal. He wasn't avoiding her—nothing of the sort. In fact, he was hardly ever out of touching distance, and it wasn't that he didn't talk to her, for he did. Sabrina didn't think anyone else was likely to notice the change, but she knew. And she was miserable.

Sabrina hadn't realized how accustomed she had become to his touch—to a hand on her arm, a fingertip sliding down her cheek, an arm brushing hers—until that contact was gone. She hadn't realized until then that his suggestive ban-

ter hadn't raised her blood pressure because she found it
annoying, but because she enjoyed the constant give-and-
take, the double meanings, the risqué exchanges.

Her reaction to the change in his attitude, she knew, was
entirely out of proportion. *Get over it, Sabrina,* she told
herself. *You'll only cause yourself more pain.*

But it was easier to recite lectures than it was to behave
accordingly. She found herself reacting to things that she'd
never noticed before—a half-smile sent her blood pound-
ing, and a hand on the back of her chair was enough to
make her skin sizzle even without the direct contact she'd
grown so used to.

By the time the evening was over, her control was hanging by an eyelash. Only sheer self-preservation allowed
Sabrina to hold on, talking all the way home about what a
nice party it had been. It was possible that her voice was
a little too high, a little too breathless, a little too fast—but
meaningless chatter was preferable to silence, and far better
than inviting a discussion of what had been going on all
evening.

Jennings opened the front door for them. Sabrina
shrugged her cape off and went to hang it up while the
butler helped Caleb out of his trench coat. "I hope you
both had a pleasant—"

"Good night, Jennings." Caleb's tone was not grim or
curt or hurried, simply matter-of-fact.

The butler didn't show a flicker of surprise. "Good night,
miss. Good night, sir." He disappeared toward the back of
the house.

As the sound of his unhurried footsteps died away, Caleb
said very softly, "Come here, Sabrina."

She braced herself. She was in for it now. He'd waited
very patiently for this opportunity, that was obvious, and
made sure that this discussion could not be interrupted.

Now he was no doubt going to explain to her that while he wouldn't mind going to bed with her, he wasn't such an idiot as to get involved with someone who took things— took *him*—so seriously....

She couldn't move. "You don't need to—" she began. "I understand...."

Caleb took two steps toward her. "It's time to pay up on that promise."

"What promise?" Her throat was tight, her voice little more than a squeak.

"The one you made with a look across a chapel tonight. And don't tell me you didn't know I got the message." He let his cane drop with a bang onto the marble floor and held out both arms. "Come here, Sabrina."

Sheer magnetism forced her toward him, even as she protested. "But—" She couldn't get her breath. "But you didn't even touch me all evening...."

A slow smile tugged at the corner of Caleb's mouth. "Don't you know why?" He slipped an arm around her shoulders, and his lips brushed her temple with fire. She shuddered, and he pulled her closer. His mouth came down on hers fiercely, and all the pain and confusion and uncertainty and desire that Sabrina had repressed for the past few hours exploded within her.

His kiss demanded surrender, but it promised in return delights that Sabrina could not begin to imagine. By the time he raised his head, his voice was rough and Sabrina's bones were smoldering. "If I'd done this when I first wanted to," he said, "we wouldn't have gone to dinner. In fact, we might not have made it out of the chapel. *That's* why I kept my hands off you."

"I thought you weren't interested." She could hardly manage a whisper.

He held her a fraction away from him. "And what do you think now?"

She was trembling, too shaken to speak.

"If you don't want this, Sabrina, if you want me to stop—tell me right now."

But the very promise of restraint was another strand of seduction wrapping around her, holding her fast. Sabrina looked straight at him and exulted in the turbulence she saw in his eyes. "Don't stop," she whispered. "Please don't stop."

He kissed her as they climbed each stair, and by the time they reached his bedroom every square inch of her was aflame with desire. Sabrina closed her eyes and held him tightly and tried to store away every instant, every sensation, every caress. But Caleb wouldn't let her think, only feel—and as each new exhilaration was succeeded by yet another, eventually Sabrina could do nothing but give herself up to a world where there was no such thing as rational thought, only passion and longing and desire...and ultimate fulfillment.

All weddings lasted too long; Caleb had always thought they could quite easily be condensed by half and be much improved. But this one—this supposedly simple, friendly, casual, nothing-formal-about-it wedding—wasn't just dragging on, it was threatening to slide into next year.

He whiled away a little time by mentally reversing the process by which Sabrina had gotten ready for the ceremony. He counted every hairpin as he took down her French twist. He savored every button down the back of the long-sleeved and high-necked black dress as he released it.

Under that almost prudish dress, he knew, was a set of lingerie so sheer it was almost nonexistent. And under that was nothing but creamy skin, silkier and more appealing than any lingerie ever manufactured....

Undressing her in his mind, he decided grumpily, was no substitute at all for the real thing. He headed across the room so he could deliberately bump into Jake. "Isn't it about time for you and Cassie to be leaving? It's a long way to Hawaii."

Jake shrugged. "We're not flying out till tomorrow."

"Still, since it's your wedding night and all—"

Jake grinned. "What's the matter? Don't tell me you're giving serious personal thought to wedding nights."

"Of course not," Caleb said irritably. "I'm missing a good game on the sports channel, that's all."

"You're missing something, all right," Jake muttered, "but I don't think it's on the sports channel. Better be careful, Caleb. Some kinds of games can be addictive."

Caleb ignored him. He crossed the room and leaned on the back of Sabrina's chair. "Are you ready to go yet?"

She didn't look at him. "As a matter of fact," she said pleasantly, "no, I'm not ready. Why don't you sit down?"

From almost directly behind him came a light laugh, and Angelique said, "And she's not about to leave till the bouquet's been thrown, I'm sure. Not that it will do you any good to catch it, Sabrina. One of the few constants in Caleb's life is his allergy to weddings." She whirled onto the dance floor with one of Tanner Electronics' department heads.

Sabrina said, "We were just talking about Austin Weaver."

Caleb's voice was cool. "What about him?" He sat down.

Across the table, Paige leaned forward. "Is he going to take the job?"

"I haven't heard a word," Caleb said. "And since I haven't gotten so much as a hint, I'm betting against it."

Paige said doubtfully, "Of course, it's only been a few days. He might still be thinking it through because it would be an awfully big move."

"So you think I shouldn't give up yet," Caleb said.

"That kind of silence might actually be positive," Sabrina speculated. "He could just be taking his time while he thinks about it."

"You sound absolutely eager for the man to come to town," Caleb said curtly.

He didn't quite recognize the emotion that sprang into her eyes. Was it watchfulness? Craftiness? Hopefulness?

He went on deliberately, "In the meantime, however, I think I should move on to interview the other candidates. You may as well start planning a couple more dinner parties."

"Mason Maxwell will be pleased about that," Sabrina said. "But surely you'll wait till Jake's back from Hawaii—right?"

"Why? He's looked at all the applications and given his opinion, and the final decision is mine, anyway. The sooner I hire, the sooner we can all stop marking time and get back to business." He looked around. "Speaking of which, isn't this damned reception ever going to end?"

Caleb's grouchy mood, Sabrina told herself, probably had nothing at all to do with her. Perhaps he was just feeling the nagging ache of a not yet healed knee. He'd certainly abused it in the last couple of days—standing at the rehearsal, even dancing at the wedding. She'd tried to talk him out of that, but he'd insisted. He had no intention of trying an exhibition fox-trot, he'd pointed out—just a slow dance. And they'd only stayed on the floor for a few minutes.

But there was no denying that something had changed his attitude. The morning's tender lover had abruptly vanished. Midway through the reception, there wasn't a hint of him left to be found. But why?

Was Angelique right that he'd simply had his fill of weddings? Sabrina didn't doubt that, in some areas, Angelique understood Caleb even better than he did himself.

Or had his mood been altered by Paige's casual question about Austin Weaver? If so, was it the reminder of the man himself that had caused the irritation, or the idea that Caleb was going to have to move on to his other candidates?

And why wasn't he going to wait till Jake returned from his honeymoon to sit in on those interviews? Was he so anxious to have the process finished?

And did that fact have anything to do with Sabrina? He'd told her to plan the parties—but he'd also made it clear that he wanted them done quickly. Did that mean he wanted to hurry the interviews along—or that he was anxious to be finished with Sabrina, too?

I always said I wasn't going to be the bimbo of the week, she thought wryly. *And sure enough, it's looking as if I won't last even that long.*

When they reached Caleb's house after the wedding reception was finally finished, there was an unfamiliar car in the driveway, and Jennings greeted them with the news that one of Tanner's engineers had been waiting for Caleb all afternoon.

Caleb muttered something that might have been an apology and limped into the living room. Sabrina told Jennings to take him a pain pill. Maybe, she thought, with a little time and rest, Caleb would get back to normal.

But down deep inside, she didn't hold out much hope.

She sat in the sunroom to sketch out the dinner parties he'd asked for, and when the phone rang almost at her elbow she answered it automatically. The voice on the other end was deep and strong and almost musical. "I'll get Caleb immediately," she managed to say, and hurried into the living room, cordless phone in hand.

Caleb broke off in the middle of a sentence about spring-powered motors. "What is it, Sabrina?"

She held out the telephone. "It's Austin Weaver."

"And he's reduced you almost to speechlessness, I see." He punched a button and said, "Hello, Weaver."

She knew she shouldn't hover; this was private. But the young engineer was still sitting there, eyes wide, and Sabrina thought mulishly that she had a lot better right to know Austin Weaver's answer than he did. For one thing, she might not have to throw those other two dinner parties....

And exactly how did she feel about that possibility? Relieved, of course; those parties were nothing to look forward to. Yet, without the parties, there would be no reason at all for her to stay. Caleb's knee was only an excuse; though he wouldn't be back on his motorcycle for a few weeks, if he could maneuver around a dance floor—even for a few minutes—he had no need of a full-time attendant. The original terms of the agreement were clear—once he was mobile again, he could take care of himself where the bimbos were concerned.

And according to his definition, Sabrina realized, she was now probably just one more bimbo to deal with.

Caleb put the telephone down. "Well—that solves a lot of problems," he said deliberately.

Sabrina frowned. "You mean.... Is he coming?"

"The first week of December."

She bit her lip.

"I thought you'd be happy at the news."

"I am," she said hastily. "It's just that—"

"That you're confused now, and you think I may try to get in your way because of last night." He pushed aside a stack of drawings and stood up. "Don't worry about that—it was quite clear to me how attracted you were to Austin Weaver. Now that he's coming, of course you'll want to be free."

So this was it, she thought. This was the way it would end—with Caleb pretending to have her best interests at heart. At least she wasn't going to have to listen to him tell her that he didn't want her any more.

"Of course," she said. Her lips felt stiff. "How wonderful of you to understand."

CHAPTER TEN

CALEB'S pencil moved across the drawing, and the young engineer frowned in concentration. Slowly, his brow cleared. "I think you've got it, sir. That's what I couldn't visualize before—right here."

Caleb tossed the pencil down and idly rubbed his aching knee. "Well, see how far you can run with it now, Eric, and let me know next week how it's going."

The young man rolled up the drawings and stood. "Thanks for seeing me on the weekend."

"I'm glad you came by. Once Weaver gets on board things will be easier during the week, but just now it's about the only time I have. You don't mind letting yourself out, I'm sure." Caleb stretched out on the couch, elevated his knee and closed his eyes. It had been a long, long day. The wedding. A nicely tangled little engineering problem. Austin Weaver. Sabrina...

He listened for the creak of the front door closing behind the young engineer and then raised his voice. "Sabrina?"

He had some fences to mend, there was no doubt about that. What had gotten into him—jabbing at her like that about Austin Weaver? Though she hadn't denied it...

But that wasn't really the point. Had he honestly expected that she'd defend herself? Not under those circumstances; Sabrina had too much class to get into a discussion in front of one of his employees. A whole lot more class than Caleb had, in fact, or he wouldn't have brought it up in the first place. Yes, he definitely had some fences to mend.

He heard the butler moving around in the front hall. "Jennings, would you ask Sabrina to come here?"

"I'm afraid that's not possible, sir. She went out about an hour ago."

"An hour ago?" Caleb stared at his wristwatch. "Have I been tied up that long? Where was she going at this time of night?"

"She did not say, sir." Jennings cleared his throat. "The indications were that she does not intend to return. She took a suitcase with her."

Caleb leaped to his feet. She couldn't do this to him. They had a deal—

"Your cane, sir," Jennings said, and handed it to him.

Caleb looked at the glossy black stick with bemusement and realized abruptly that he'd paced the width of the room without it—and without noticing. Now that he was paying attention, he realized that there was more than a twinge of pain in his knee—but he hadn't collapsed in agony as he would have done a few days ago.

Yes, they'd had a deal—she'd stay till he was well enough to be on his own. Obviously Sabrina thought that time had come, and considering what he'd just managed to do, Caleb couldn't exactly argue the point.

But to walk out on him without saying goodbye, without even a word of explanation—

Or did she think she'd explained everything she needed to? What was the last thing she'd said to him? He'd made his crack about how attracted she was to Austin Weaver. And she'd said, *How wonderful of you to understand.* Something like that, at any rate.

So that was the answer. His instinct had been right, after all. And if that was the way she felt about it—about him and about Austin Weaver—he wouldn't even want her to stick around. If she didn't want him, then he didn't want her—

Yes, I do, he thought. *I want her more than I've ever wanted anything before.*

He shook his head in confusion. Where had that come from? It was insane, really. There had always been such a ready supply of women who were attracted to him that he'd never bothered to look beyond them at the ones who might not be. Could he possibly be dangling after a woman who didn't even care what he thought, what he wanted? The very idea was ludicrous.

Perhaps, he thought, he was just miffed because he hadn't been the one who called a halt, because Sabrina had left him instead of the other way around.

He'd said something once, carelessly, about not asking women to move in with him because it was so difficult and messy to get them to move out. Well, Sabrina hadn't served him up with that problem. It had been very thoughtful of her, in fact, to clear out without making a scene.

Except he wasn't inclined to feel in the least grateful, because he hadn't been ready for her to go. Not nearly ready.

So what was he going to do about it?

Sabrina saw Paige's minivan pull up in front of the condo, and she seized her coat and handbag and ran out to climb in. "We should finish up this project by noon, shouldn't we?" she asked as cheerfully as she could.

Paige nodded. "There are at least three loads of clothes and household stuff, and several different charities Jayne wants them delivered to, but then our part of the job will be done. I have to admit that disposing of an entire household has been a lot more work than I expected. It seemed like such a simple job when Cassie took it on."

"At least Cassie will be back before the holiday rush starts. We should have another couple of weeks of peace and quiet before we get swamped with Christmas preparations.''

Paige shook her head. ''With Cassie taking time off even before the wedding, it's already gotten crazy.''

''And having me occupied with Caleb hasn't helped,'' Sabrina admitted. It felt odd, saying his name as if nothing had changed.

''Neither has the fact that my mother scheduled a string of doctor's appointments this month. She can't help it, of course, and normally the timing would have been all right, but I'm going to have to juggle my calendar as it is. Was it really just a few weeks ago when we were desperate for business, the cash flow looked so weak that you even offered to ask your father for a loan, and the Tanner Electronics contract looked like manna from heaven? Now I wonder if we should have taken it on at all. If the holiday rush picks up as I think it might this year—''

If Paige was already having doubts about Tanner, Sabrina thought, maybe it wouldn't matter so much after all if Caleb retaliated and canceled the contract because Sabrina had walked out on him. Of course, she reminded herself, he wasn't likely to retaliate; only angry people did that, and Caleb was no doubt more relieved to be rid of her than furious because she'd gone.

''When it comes to contracts,'' Sabrina said, ''I suppose the new CEO will have ideas of his own. You were right, by the way, about Austin Weaver taking his time to consider. He's coming.''

The minivan swerved. ''Damn,'' Paige said. ''There's always somebody on the road who thinks it's their right to take up both lanes. What about Caleb? It was his idea in the first place, and he'll still be the boss.''

''I doubt he'd interfere in that kind of decision. He'll have to give the man some authority if he expects to keep him.'' ·

Paige stopped for a red light. "I tried to reach you at Caleb's house this morning," she said casually, "before I called the condo."

"I thought you might have." Sabrina tried to keep her voice matter-of-fact.

"Don't want to talk about it?"

"What is there to talk about? It's over."

"I'm sorry, sweetheart."

Sabrina forced herself to smile. "But not too sorry, I suspect. You gave me your opinion up front—and you were right."

"Yes, but..." Paige shook her head. "At the wedding, there was something about the way Caleb was looking at you that made me think you weren't just one of a series to him."

Sabrina would have given anything to be able to believe that Paige had been right, but she couldn't. As a general rule, Paige was pretty perceptive—but she'd misread the signals that time.

Once Caleb had even told her that she was one of a kind. But in fact, she didn't stand out at all. She wasn't one of a kind, just one of a series...and not even an important one.

Sabrina had apparently packed up in a hurry, for she'd left small possessions scattered all over his house. A lipstick tube on the bathroom shelf. A hair clip on the coffee table. A sheer black nylon under the edge of his bed...

Caleb ran his fingertips over the cool nylon, but what he felt was the warm, silky skin of Sabrina's leg as he'd released the stocking from its fastener. Irritated at himself, he dropped the stocking into the wastebasket. What was the matter with him, anyway? He'd never lost his concentration over a woman before.

But she's not just a woman. She's Sabrina, his conscience whispered. *She's different....*

Oh, she was different, all right, he gibed. Nobody else had ever knocked him down, cracked up his knee, wrapped a paint-soaked towel around his head.... He should have run while he had the chance. But he hadn't—and that, for a man whose sense of self-preservation was incredibly strong, was certainly an odd reaction.

And now it was too late.

He knew where he'd gone wrong, of course. Her total capitulation had been incredibly satisfying, and the idea of having her waiting on him, after what she'd done, had fed his vanity. And the whole concept of immunity had been an eminently sensible one—how could he possibly be blinded by her beauty, when he knew from firsthand experience how dangerous she could be?

But it wasn't her outer beauty that had caused the trouble, it was the loveliness that lay inside her. And while he'd been wasting time trying to protect his body, the damage she'd done was far more than physical. His knee would be as good as new in a few more weeks, but it would take decades to get over the rest—if, indeed, he could recuperate at all. Sober consideration told him it was unlikely.

Standing firm in the face of overwhelming odds was not courage, he remembered telling her, it was sheer idiocy. But it wasn't flight he was contemplating now. It was complete and abject surrender. Of course, he couldn't present it to Sabrina quite like that.

And then there was the problem of presenting it at all; he'd messed up royally, and he wouldn't be surprised if she didn't even want to talk to him. So he'd have to find a way.

Abruptly, he realized he was stroking the stocking again. He didn't even know how it had gotten from the wastebasket into his hand, and he didn't care. He just knew that the black stocking would have to do for a little while—until he had her to hold, instead.

* * *

The elderly man fussed around the kitchen till Sabrina's nerves were on edge, insisting on handing her each dirty dish in turn. She reminded herself of what Paige had said about him and tried to relax. Maybe Ben Orcutt *was* just lonely, and his awkwardly flirtatious approaches were simply his way of being friendly.

"I'm glad you didn't let the dishes stack up so long this time, Ben," she said as she submerged the last stack of recycled plastic plates in the soapy water. "It's not even two weeks since Cassie was here, is it?"

"You're not done already, are you?" He sounded anxious.

"Almost. But think of it this way—the job doesn't take as long each time, but we'll come more often."

The telephone rang, and Sabrina jumped and splashed the dishwater. She didn't think she'd ever heard it ring before in any of the multitude of times she'd been in Ben Orcutt's apartment. Was it her imagination, or was he approaching it warily himself?

After a moment, he cupped a hand over the receiver. "It's for you," he said, and Sabrina dried off her rubber-gloved hands.

"I had to call Paige to get a rundown of where you might be," Eileen McDermott said sharply, "and I've phoned half a dozen people at least, looking for you. You might try to remember, Sabrina, that there's a reason Rent-A-Wife pays a fee every month for that cell phone you carry."

"Sorry," Sabrina said. "I've been without it for so long while it was being repaired that I forgot to turn it on today."

Eileen sniffed. "I suppose, now that you're involved with that man, your mind will turn to mush just like Cassie's did."

Sabrina bit her tongue. Even if Eileen's information was a bit behind the times, her comment was still very nearly true—Sabrina had been forgetting things all week, and the problem didn't seem to be getting any better just because the days since she'd seen Caleb were starting to add up. She said sweetly, "I'm sure, since Mr. Orcutt is paying for my time, that you didn't call just to chat, Eileen."

"Of course not. Someone left a phone number on the answering machine, with a request for you to call back."

"I'll get to it first thing tomorrow."

"Perhaps you should take care of it tonight. He didn't say it was urgent, but I've spent the better part of an hour trying to locate you."

Sabrina swore under her breath. Then she reminded herself that she really had nothing else to do, anyway. The busier she kept herself now, the better off she'd be. In fact, she might as well work all weekend; it would serve the dual purpose of knocking down the waiting list and occupying her mind so she didn't have time to think about how different last weekend had been. There was no point in recalling the empty memories of one glorious but ultimately meaningless night.

She jotted down the number and suggested to Eileen—with a slightly malicious note in her voice—that since she had interrupted Ben Orcutt's expensive hour of service perhaps Eileen, too, should apologize to him, and handed the phone to Ben.

The remaining dishes were quickly disposed of, after their extra soaking, and Sabrina had finished cleaning up before Ben was off the telephone. Paige was definitely right about Ben being lonely, she concluded. The poor soul had actually been trying to flirt with Eileen!

In her car, she unearthed her cell phone from the depths of the leather bag that served as her mobile office. A deep masculine voice answered.

Not Caleb's, of course, she thought as she listened absently to the man on the other end of the line. But then it had been stupid to think that Caleb might be trying to get hold of her. And it was stupider yet to think that if he did, he'd go out of his way to leave a number that she wouldn't recognize and so wouldn't hesitate to call....

But this really wasn't fair, she thought. Didn't she have enough trouble already, without Austin Weaver asking her for help?

When Jennings answered the front door, Sabrina wasn't surprised at how startled he seemed to be at the sight of her. She noted the way his gaze darted almost involuntarily toward the living room, and she said pleasantly, "I'm sure Caleb doesn't want to see me, but then I don't want to see him, either. I just don't have a choice in the matter, because it's business. So unless he has a bimbo drum and bugle corps dancing attendance on him, I'll wait till he's free."

Jennings stepped back from the door. "I'll tell him you're here, miss."

Sabrina paced the hall for a moment, stopping at the dining room door long enough to note that the furniture she'd rented was still there.

From across the hallway, Caleb said softly, "Business?"

Sabrina spun around.

He looked taller, she thought. That was probably because he wasn't relying on either a cane or a crutch; his knee might still be wrapped under his black trousers, but it was obviously much improved. And he looked different—as if months had passed since she'd seen him, instead of three days minus a few odd hours.

It had been difficult enough, these last few days, to deal with suddenly being alone when she'd grown so used to spending most of her time with him. But now, when she saw him again, her heart ached. If she had still cherished the fragment of a doubt over how she felt about him, that one long look across an almost-echoing front hall would have given her the answer.

Caleb spoke again. "Business, you said."

The soft words dragged her back to reality. He was the man she loved, the man she would always love—and the man she could not have. But if Sabrina was to maintain any dignity at all, she must not let him see how much the mere sight of him could affect her.

She cleared her throat. "Austin Weaver called me today."

Caleb merely looked inquisitive.

As if, she thought, he believed her announcement was a form of boasting—an attempt to make him aware that even if he didn't want her any more, she was still desirable to someone else. As if she was such a fool.

"And were you happy to hear from him?" Caleb asked.

"Not particularly. He called because he wants Rent-A-Wife to find him a place to live, among other things—and he asked to speak to me because he knows Cassie's in Hawaii, and he's never met Paige."

"Your sales pitch is very effective," Caleb murmured. "Congratulations."

"And the reason that I'm here now—"

"You're surely not asking my permission to take on a client."

"In a way I am, since you're going to be paying at least part of the bill." She took a deep breath. "He told me the discussion of his executive perks had been somewhat vague and suggested I call you to find out exactly how much you're prepared to spend. And, I suppose, exactly what's included. Housing? Car? Jet? Private school for his daughter? Personal chef?"

"All of them interesting ideas," Caleb said. "Come and sit down, Sabrina."

"Can't you just give me enough specifics so I can get started?"

He had turned toward the living room. "You seem anxious."

"No, I'm busy. You must have a list in mind, and a figure."

Caleb shook his head. "Not that I can just rattle off the top of my head. Anyway, I need to rest my knee, and I asked Jennings to make coffee for us. Come in."

Reluctantly, she followed him into the living room, where a fire was burning cheerfully. She felt a bit shivery, but Sabrina knew that wasn't the chill of the autumn air but of the situation. Just being in the same room with him again set off all kinds of memories.

Deliberately, she pushed them aside and said, "So it really was vague? The discussion of perks, I mean."

"I suppose you could call it that. Why?"

"Because it doesn't make any sense that the two of you—hardheaded as you both are—wouldn't have nailed down the details before you made an agreement. When Austin suggested that I start asking questions, I thought perhaps he was trying to renegotiate."

"To get a better deal from me by using you."

There was an ironic note in his voice, and it set Sabrina's nerves on edge. "Why not? I'm not as odd a choice as a bargainer as I might seem, Caleb. Or do you mean he's just behind the times—thinking that I'm still your girl and therefore can talk you out of anything?"

"Oh, I'm sure he knows better than that."

Her eyes narrowed. "And just how does he know?"

"Because I brought him up to date, of course."

Fury built to a slow furnace deep in the pit of her stomach. "Now that's interesting—the two of you left the discussion of compensation to take care of itself so you could talk about me. Or maybe I'm one of the perks you were talking about. Housing, car, jet, private school, personal chef—and mistress?''

"You're getting a little carried away, Sabrina."

"I knew I was just one of a series to you, Caleb, but I thought I was a little more important than a baseball card to trade off to Austin Weaver because you're tired of me!''

She broke off, embarrassed, as Jennings came in, carrying a silver tray. Automatically, Sabrina began to clear a corner of the coffee table, which was stacked higher than she'd seen it before with newspapers, magazines, boxes and gift bags. As she shifted a box, it tipped off the edge of the table, and the contents spilled onto the carpet.

Her anger gave way; almost reluctantly she started to laugh. "Red satin panties?''

Caleb stepped forward to take the coffee tray from Jennings, and at his nod the butler silently retreated.

"The bimbos are sending you red satin panties? Well, it didn't take long for your life to get back to normal, did it? I told you they'd come after you with a vengeance as soon as I was gone.''

Caleb set the tray in the gap on the coffee table. "I miss you, Sabrina.''

The raspy note in his voice felt like a saw cutting her feet out from under her. Unable to stand any longer, Sabrina dropped into a deep leather chair. Determined that she would not let him see he was getting to her, she willed her hand not to tremble as she reached for a steaming cup from the tray.

All right, so he misses me, she told herself. *It doesn't mean anything more than that.* "You just miss having a bodyguard. You know what's the matter with you, Caleb? You only want what you can't have. The one thing that makes me different from every other woman in your life is that *I* walked out on *you.*" She set her cup on the tray and slid to the edge of her chair. "Tell you what, Caleb. I can't do anything about Austin's problem till tomorrow, anyway, so you think about it—''

He put out a hand as if to stop her. She drew back, and his fingertips caught the sleeve of her herringbone jacket and pulled it up just enough to reveal a slim streak of platinum on her wrist. "You're wearing my bracelet," he said.

My bracelet—as if wearing it branded her as his property, she thought irritably. "Why shouldn't I? I earned it. Besides, it goes well with the jacket. I'll call you at the office in the morning." She stood up.

He got to his feet, as well. "You can't wait to get out of here, can you? Just like Saturday night, when you left without a word."

"You seemed to have said everything there was to say."

He shook his head. "Oh, no. I hardly even got a good start. Of course, it wasn't till after you were gone that I realized what I wanted to tell you. I want you back, Sabrina. And I'm going to do whatever it takes to convince you."

Stunned, Sabrina turned too quickly and lost her footing. She staggered into Caleb, hitting him squarely in the chest. He put out an arm as he went down—to save her from falling? to brace himself?—but only succeeded in pulling her along with him as he fell onto the deeply cushioned leather couch.

She was cradled against him, chest to chest, and her first effort to break free only pressed her more closely against him. "Do you think this is going to convince me?" she asked tartly.

Caleb's hands tightened on her upper arms, and he dragged her higher against him till she was staring into his eyes. "Oh, hell," he said. "There's no point in trying to talk to you when you're in this frame of mind. What have I got to lose, anyway?" His hand slid to the back of her neck and pulled her down to him.

His kiss held a desperate recklessness that seemed to reach straight through Sabrina and squeeze her heart. She had never expected to be so close to him again, and she could no more have denied herself than she could have stepped out of her skin.

He kissed her till she couldn't breathe, till her bones felt like taffy on a hot summer's day. And even then he didn't let her go; instead, he twisted a little, turning onto his side, and suddenly Sabrina was caught between his body and the back of the couch, even less able to move than before.

His eyes were darker than she'd ever seen them, except for a gleam that could only be triumph. He'd done exactly what he had set out to do, she realized with a sinking sensation. He had made it clear that he wanted her. And he had forced her to admit that she wanted him every bit as much.

But that was all. Nothing had changed, except that she'd given herself away. Even what he'd said about wanting her back didn't really mean anything. He still felt desire—or perhaps it was just pique that he hadn't been the one to call a halt to their affair—but there was no telling how long that would last.

"Let me go," she said.

"No. You got yourself into this, and now at least you're going to listen to me."

Sabrina tried to wriggle away, but he tightened his hold, pressing her closer against him and threatening to set her skin on fire. "So talk," she muttered. "What is it you wanted to tell me?"

Caleb took a deep breath. "After you smashed up my knee, I had no intention of ever being within a hundred yards of you again. That much I'm perfectly clear about—it was after that when things started getting fuzzy. I know I kept on thinking about you and telling myself you were on my mind only because I was furious at you. Then you came to see me, and before I knew it I was blackmailing you into being my nursemaid, bodyguard and girl Friday.''

"You seemed to know exactly what you were doing that day—as if you'd planned it all out. Right down to being immune.''

"The only thing I can figure out,'' he said, "is that by the time I swore I was immune to you, I wasn't any more. Not that I'd have admitted it. Not that I even knew it. I just knew I didn't want you to go away.''

It wasn't everything she wanted—but it was a whole lot more than Sabrina had ever dreamed of. If he cared at all for her...

Don't get ahead of yourself, she thought. *Don't start hearing what you want to hear, instead of what he's really saying.*

"I thought for a while it was just good old-fashioned lust,'' Caleb went on. "I even believed that explained why I was ready to bite Austin Weaver any time you smiled at him. I didn't realize for a long time that I actually wasn't jealous of Austin.''

She frowned and had to admit to a thread of disappointment. If he had cared at all, surely he'd have been jealous. He'd *acted* jealous.

"I was afraid of him, instead,'' Caleb said. His voice was husky. "He seemed to be your type somehow, classy and cultured and lots of things that I'm not, and I was afraid that you would find him attractive.'' He sighed. "You see, I didn't expect love to hurt, Sabrina—that's partly why I didn't recognize it when it hit me.''

Love? She forgot to breathe.

"I thought my knee was painful till I realized what you'd done to my heart. You took it and you stamped on it and you walked out on me. And only then did I finally face up to the fact that I'd fallen in love with you.''

She was having trouble taking it all in. *You're really*

here, she told herself. *You're not delusional. He's really saying these things.*

"And now I suppose the question is what you're going to do about it," Caleb said. "There isn't a reason in the world why you should care about me, Sabrina. I've been a fool. I've treated you badly. I've got a rotten track record, and I got off to the worst start imaginable with you. And yet the way you kissed me just now... You might not love me, but you couldn't do that if you wanted someone else more." He cupped a hand under her chin and said, with new determination, "I've never told any woman I love her, Sabrina—except my mother. Not till now. I don't know how to prove to you that I'm telling the truth, but I am going to convince you."

There was an edge to his voice that she'd never heard before. She stared into the almost somber depths of his eyes, and inside her a tight little knot started to unravel.

"I believe you," she whispered. "And I think that I could find a few reasons to care about you."

She could see the tension slowly drain out of him, and she could feel the new looseness and ease in every muscle in his body as he held her closer. This time his kiss wasn't desperate, it was gentle, almost tranquil. Still, underneath lay a hint of the same recklessness he'd shown earlier, and she knew that whatever was in store for them, it wasn't likely to be altogether peaceful. And no matter how gentle he was, he could still leave her breathless.

"I didn't know what was happening to me, either," she confessed. "I've grown so tired of men who only see my body, not my brain—men like Mason Maxwell, and my father, who thought the only job I was fit for was hanging admiringly on some man's arm. You seemed to be just like them, Caleb, thinking I was one more bimbo, and sending me out to play while you talked business. And yet I couldn't simply ignore you as I wanted to do. You made me laugh, and you made me hungry for you.... I thought it would kill me, having to admit that I'd fallen in love with you."

He nibbled the soft skin of her throat, and she arched her neck like a satisfied kitten and reveled in his touch.

"What would you have done," she asked finally, "if I hadn't come tonight, Caleb?"

"I don't know. I was trying to work out a new plan when you finally showed up." He turned his attention to the sensitive hollow at the base of her throat. "Maybe I'd have demanded that you finish the redecorating you started."

"I'd have finished, all right. I'd have painted your bedroom purple and filled it with ruffles." Sabrina frowned. "Wait a minute. What do you mean, you were working out a new plan? You expected me to come?"

"Let's say I did my best to provide you a reason. Austin didn't mind playing along, because he'd been thinking of asking Rent-A-Wife for help anyway, so—"

She pulled away, bracing her hands against his chest. "You *ordered* him to call me?"

"Not at all," Caleb said with dignity. "I asked him very nicely. But when all day went by and you didn't come, I'd just about concluded that you'd seen through the smoke screen—as you did, of course. That was the weak spot of the plan—the idea that we hadn't settled all the executive perks—and you caught it right away."

She shook her head. "Not exactly. It just seemed strange, that's all. I never dreamed...." *That you cared enough to go to the trouble,* she thought, and a delicious shiver ran through her as she sank against him. "Now you've made me curious, Caleb. What's the real story on Austin's executive perks?"

"Whatever Austin wants, Austin gets. As far as I'm concerned, he's earned it just by making you show up here. But the hell with executive perks—I really don't want to talk about them right now, when there are a lot better things to do." He kissed her gently. "So when are you going to marry me, Sabrina?"

The glow that had been building deep inside her had grown as warm as the sun. But there was still a fragment of doubt deep inside. "Are you sure you want to go quite that far? You compared a wedding to—let me think. Being turned into hamburger on a football field, I think that was it."

"Do you remember every idiotic thing I ever said?"

"Most of them."

"And you'll no doubt be throwing them in my face for the rest of my life."

She was suddenly serious. "Do you mean that, Caleb? Really? The rest of your life?"

"More than I've ever meant anything before," he said huskily. "I want it all, Sabrina. You, and marriage, and kids, and forever. And if you're still worried about being just one of a series... Well, you are, darling. You're the last one. The ultimate one. The only important one."

She smiled, and kissed him very slowly, and put her head against his shoulder so she could listen to the steady thumping of his heart.

It's hard to resist the lure of the Australian Outback

One of Harlequin Romance's best-loved Australian authors

Margaret Way

brings you

Look for

A WIFE AT KIMBARA (#3595)
March 2000

THE BRIDESMAID'S WEDDING (#3607)
June 2000

THE ENGLISH BRIDE (#3619)
September 2000

Available at your favorite retail outlet.

Visit us at www.romance.net

HROUT

Looking For More Romance?

Visit Romance.net

Look us up on-line at: http://www.romance.net

Check in daily for these and other exciting features:

Hot off the press

View all current titles, and purchase them on-line.

What do the stars have in store for you?

Horoscope

Hot deals

Exclusive offers available only at Romance.net

Plus, don't miss our interactive quizzes, contests and bonus gifts.

PWEB

HARLEQUIN®
Makes any time special™

HARLEQUIN®
AMERICAN ◆ ROMANCE®

WANTS TO SEND YOU
HOME FOR THE HOLIDAYS!

AmericanAirlines®

LOOK FOR CONTEST DETAILS
COMING NEXT MONTH IN ALL
HARLEQUIN
AMERICAN ROMANCE®
SERIES BOOKS!

OR ONLINE AT
www.eHarlequin.com/homefortheholidays

For complete rules and entry form send a
self-addressed stamped envelope (residents of
Washington or Vermont may omit return postage)
to "Harlequin Home for the Holidays Contest
9119 Rules" (in the U.S.) P.O. Box 9069, Buffalo,
NY 14269-9069, (in Canada) P.O. Box 637,
Fort Erie, ON, Canada L2A 5X3.

HARHFTH1

Romance is just one click away!

online book **serials**

➤ *Exclusive* to our web site, get caught up in both the daily and weekly online installments of new romance stories.

➤ Try the Writing Round Robin. Contribute a chapter to a story created by our members. Plus, winners will get prizes.

romantic **travel**

➤ Want to know where the best place to kiss in New York City is, or which restaurant in Los Angeles is the most romantic? Check out our Romantic Hot Spots for the scoop.

➤ Share your travel tips and stories with us on the romantic travel message boards.

romantic reading **library**

➤ Relax as you read our collection of Romantic Poetry.

➤ Take a peek at the Top 10 Most Romantic Lines!

Visit us online at

www.eHarlequin.com

on Women.com Networks

HEUT1

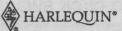 **HARLEQUIN®**

Harlequin Romance®

Coming Next Month

#3607 THE BRIDESMAID'S WEDDING Margaret Way
When Ally Kinross and Rafe Cameron meet again at her brother's
wedding, the attraction between them is as powerful as ever. But
their love affair six years ago ended unhappily, and this time Rafe is
determined not to get hurt....

Legends of the Outback

#3608 WIFE ON APPROVAL Leigh Michaels
Paige was shocked to see Austin again. It was seven years since she'd
called him "husband"—now he was only a client! Except he wanted
to give their marriage another try...or did he just want a mother for
the little girl now in his care?

Hiring Ms. Right

#3609 THE BOSS'S BRIDE Emma Richmond
Claris was Adam Turmaine's assistant, but her job description had
temporarily changed. And if being a stand-in mom was demanding,
then living with her boss was equally so—even if he was irresistibly
attractive....

Marrying the Boss

#3610 PROJECT: DADDY Patricia Knoll
Paris Barbour could see that Mac Weston adored the two children
who had been unexpectedly left in his care—he just didn't know
how to show it! As the new nanny, she was determined to help him
learn to be a daddy—and possibly a husband, too....

Baby Boom